All She Wanted To Do Was Cry...

"Thank you," Stephanie said quietly.

"For what?"

"For being there with me this afternoon, with Jeff. You've always been a good father to him. If I've never said that to you before..." Her upper lip was quivering.

He leaned against the wall, drawing her to him. "You know, you wouldn't get sick to your stomach if you'd cry when you need to," Alex said.

"Oh, shut up. I don't *want* to cry."

"It's good for you," Alex coaxed.

"It isn't."

"Here." He dug a handkerchief from his pocket. "Blow."

"No."

"Can you breathe now?"

"Yes," she said crossly.

"Good, because I'm going to kiss you."

She ducked, fast.

Alex was faster, his mouth capturing hers swiftly. Sensations floated through her—desire, loneliness, an echo of something terribly powerful.

Dear Reader,

Welcome to Silhouette! Our goal is to give you hours of unbeatable reading pleasure, and we hope you'll enjoy each month's six new Silhouette Desires. These sensual, provocative love stories are both believable and compelling—sometimes they're poignant, sometimes humorous, but always enjoyable.

Indulge yourself. Experience all the passion and excitement of falling in love along with our heroine as she meets the irresistible man of her dreams and together they overcome all obstacles in the path to a happy ending.

If this is your first Desire, I hope it'll be the first of many. If you're already a Silhouette Desire reader, thanks for your support! Look for some of your favorite authors in the coming months: Stephanie James, Diana Palmer, Dixie Browning, Ann Major and Doreen Owens Malek, to name just a few.

Happy reading!

Isabel Swift
Senior Editor

SDRL-7/85

JENNIFER GREENE
Foolish Pleasure

Silhouette Desire

Published by Silhouette Books New York

America's Publisher of Contemporary Romance

SILHOUETTE BOOKS
300 East 42nd St., New York, N.Y. 10017

ISBN: 0-373-05293-6

First Silhouette Books printing July 1986

America's Publisher of Contemporary Romance

Printed in the U.S.A.

Books by Jennifer Greene

Silhouette Desire

Body and Soul #263
Foolish Pleasure #293

JENNIFER GREENE

lives near Lake Michigan. Born in Grosse Pointe, she moved to a farm when she married her husband fifteen years ago. Jennifer feels that love needs both laughter and tribulations to grow. She's won the *Romantic Times* award for Sensuality and the RWA Silver Medallion. She also writes under the name of Jeanne Grant.

One

Number 17 on your list, ladies and gentlemen. A 1750s kneehole chest, made of mahogany and white pine. Isn't it marvelous? Note the original brass, the secret latch in the cupboard section designed to hide valuables...the craftsmanship is superb. In all honesty, the item is priceless, and I hate to start the bidding as low as five hundred...."

The crowd was large, even for an estate auction this size. Hands darted in the air, wooed either by the piece up for bid or the persuasive power of the auctioneer. Stephanie's boss claimed she had just a smidgeon of con artist in her soul, an offensive comment on her character that she thoroughly resented and knew was true. Cheating—never, but she knew the allure of wanting the forbidden. From there it was a simple matter of coaxing people that whatever she was selling was uniquely desirable, and she did it with a sassy flash of blue eyes, a husky alto, a hint of promise in her smile.

At least most days. This particular afternoon, the auction was running late. Everything that could possibly go wrong had done so, and George was determined to wave yet another piece of paper at her from the sidelines.

"Sold!" Stephanie discreetly snapped down the gavel, winked her congratulations at the new owner and quickly stepped down to face her boss. George was bald and nearing sixty. He dressed like an undertaker, thrived on efficiency and could just occasionally be a hand-wringer. She reached for the slip of paper in his hand, murmuring a soothing, "All right. What now?"

"Brace yourself, Stephanie."

She smiled, resisting the urge to pat his bare head. "So we've got one more little crisis to handle... nothing new since we took on this estate." Her face paled abruptly as she scanned the piece of paper. Fear slashed through her veins in the tick of a second.

"When your housekeeper couldn't reach you at the office, she called the police. She didn't want you to panic, Stephanie, and the accident wasn't necessarily that serious, but they took your son to Hitchcock Hospital."

It took ten minutes to hand the price and items list to George, find a phone to call the hospital, dart through the crowd and wedge her modest Le Baron through the lot of packed Mercedes and BMWs and get on the main road. She was an hour from Hanover. An hour from home. An hour from her fourteen-year-old son, who at three o'clock on a Friday afternoon in October should be just arriving home from school on his bike. Not lying in a hospital bed. Not Jeff.

The hospital couldn't—or wouldn't—tell her anything over the phone, except that Jeff was taken care of, and that they'd tried to contact both her and the boy's father. For a second she almost told them to forget the boy's father; Alex lived in New York. But of course he didn't. A few months before he'd moved back to Boston, a fact she simply kept forgetting.

She wound in and around traffic like a madwoman, her foot as heavy as lead on the accelerator, acid twisting in her stomach at the thought of anything happening to Jeff. It had to be a mistake. All she had to do was look around.... Leaves were just starting to turn color on a lazy autumn day; the sun was out; she crossed the Connecticut River as she'd crossed it a zillion times. Everything was normal, how could anything possibly be wrong with Jeff?

Stephanie parked in a no-parking zone directly in front of the emergency-room door, well aware she risked her car being towed. They could tow it. They could have it. As long as Jeff was all right.

A harried-looking young nurse manned the front desk. An old man with a makeshift bandage on his arm, then a frantic mother holding a wailing baby, were ahead of Stephanie. When it was Stephanie's turn, the nurse glanced up with a flash of relief in her smile. With one look she realized that the slim graceful woman wasn't the type to get hysterical.

Stephanie knew exactly the image she presented. Her champagne hair was slicked back in a French coil; her coral linen suit was spotless, and nature had given her a naturally patrician profile that revealed no emotion if she didn't let it. Her stomach was churning steel wool, but no one could know it because her low voice was calm and controlled.

"I'm Mrs. Carson. You have my son, Jeff. I was told he was brought in here—"

"Yes." The nurse checked her roster. "I'm afraid he's still in with the doctor—"

"May I see him?"

"When he's through being examined, of course. I'm afraid there were several others ahead of him; it may be a little time yet."

Stephanie's nails dug into her palm. A little time? What could possibly be taking more time? She'd already wasted an hour in getting here. The swell of nausea was so overwhelming she could barely talk. "Can you tell me what happened? How badly he's hurt, how—"

"Really, I promise the doctor will be with you shortly. We've had several other accidents this afternoon, Mrs. Carson...."

There was a waiting room. Stephanie parked herself by the door she believed the doctor would come through. Two minutes dragged to ten. A thousand images darted through her mind. Walking Jeff to school that first day, and crying her eyes out when he went through that kindergarten door. His first black eye—he'd gotten in a fight with a seven-year-old across the street and she'd decked him. He'd been six then, a swaggering six just like his father, with his father's same dark eyes and sassy grin. And yes, he knew better than to hit a girl but she'd called him a smartie pants.

Nausea came in spurts, like the up and down of a roller coaster. Each time the door opened Stephanie could feel her heart drop like a puddle at her feet. She could mentally hear Jeff's voice, crackling up and down the scales now that it was changing. Since puberty, he was becoming disturbingly inclined to slam doors in a mood, and when she reached out to hug him she'd get that so disgusted "Aw, Mom."

She touched icy fingers to her temples.

Her head shot up suddenly, and the pulse in her throat tripped a beat. The man bolting through the front hospital doors was dressed in jeans, work boots and a frayed dark shirt. He looked as if he'd just climbed out from the underworkings of a car—and he probably had. It wouldn't have mattered if he'd been dressed in navy-blue suit and starched shirt—at his best, Alex's thick dark hair would still manage to look mussed and shaggy; there would always be a spot of dirt on his shirt somewhere. Dirt flew at Alex. Life flew at Alex.

At seventeen, she'd been fascinated by the grease under his fingernails. She'd been fascinated by Alex, period. This was a *man,* a physical, lusty man who lived by his hands, who shouted his laughter, who seduced with earthy exhilaration. He had changed very little in fourteen years. He wasn't exceptionally tall but he was muscular, with power in his shoulders and in the snap of his dark eyes. His square features were still sun-weathered and strong, his thick black hair still looked finger-brushed and he continued to remind her of a cross between lightning and dynamite. His eyes whipped around the room and, when they saw her, stilled.

She strode toward him without hesitation. He'd told her once that they'd never manage to be friends. As in many other things Alex was dead wrong. For fourteen years she'd made sure they had a civilized divorce. A woman might jettison honesty, but never pride. Alex couldn't very well brawl when she kept on smiling, and no one knew they'd fought like cats and dogs years before. No one would guess to look at Stephanie that she'd ever fought with anyone. She was raised to elegance, not barroom shouting matches. No other man had ever roused her to throwing things like a two-year-old in a tantrum—or coaxed her into bed at first meeting with a devilish smile.

One could be damned stupid at seventeen. Now Stephanie was a long way from seventeen, but for just that moment she was having trouble maintaining her usual civilized-divorce smile. Alex looked as drawn and strained as she felt. A lifetime ago she'd made a baby with this man, and for one idiotic second she could feel her house of emotional cards tumbling down. If their marriage had been a Grade B horror story, she still knew he'd move heaven and earth for Jeff.

There was a time she believed he'd move heaven and earth for her. Steel wool and acid suddenly blended in her stomach. She had to force her chin up.

Alex ruthlessly scanned her from head to toe before halting inches away. He could smell the palest whiff of roses, see the utter perfection of her skin. The coral-colored suit tastefully complimented her leggy champagne looks, delicate cheekbones and proud chin... the word was class. This classy lady was getting more beautiful every year. This classy lady cultivated perfection, achieved it and inevitably made him want to do something rash, like take down her hair or yell at her. It made him want to rub a little dirt on her hands, or take her to bed, hard and fast, and rip past all those images.

But he'd done all that, a long time ago.

One of these years he was going to manage to feel indifferent toward her. Anger was as expensive as old memories, and looking at her now he felt an old twist of unwilling pain for the time when they'd conceived their son. Her tilted-up chin didn't fool him at all. Alex had known her far too long. He saw the elegance. He also saw the glaze of control in her eyes, the imperceptible touch of her slim hand to her stomach.

His ex-lady was close to throwing up.

He grabbed her arm, steered her to a quiet corner of the waiting room. "All right. How bad?"

She shook free from those steely fingers, but her lips were suddenly trembling. She'd been fine until he walked in. "I don't know! Alex, I can't get any answers. He has to have been in there a long time before I got here—"

"Wait here. And sit down, for heaven's sake."

She couldn't sit. She couldn't even breathe for the worry over Jeff. A few yards away, the nurse looked up when Alex leaned over the desk. The young woman first shook her head, but then Stephanie watched a coaxing smile spread across his face. Alex's smile was also Jeff's smile, a winsome bit of devil and sheer male.

Stephanie didn't care if he seduced the woman on the hospital linoleum as long as he brought back some answers. In seconds, he did. "It'll only be a few more minutes. There were three accidents ahead of him— Lord knows, it was enough to throw this small town hospital into a general state of emergency—but the fact is, they take the critical cases first. Jeff wasn't critical. He's bruised up; at the very worst a broken leg—"

"A broken leg!"

His hands clamped on her arms again, gently pushing her into the chair. "A broken leg isn't the end of the world. Calm down."

"I *am* calm," she snapped. Anyone else in the room could see she was completely calm and in perfect control. "I still don't understand why I can't see him...."

She couldn't because the nurse had told Alex that Jeff wasn't in the best of shape when they'd brought him in, something he wasn't about to tell Stephanie. He dropped heavily into the chair next to her, with pictures in his mind that he wished he could erase.

They were both silent. Stephanie stared at the wall. "You're probably blaming me," Stephanie said in a low voice. "*I'm* blaming me. I should have been home. Alex, I'm almost always home when he comes home from school...."

"An accident is no one's fault."

"I should never have let him ride his bike from school—"

"It's a quiet town with quiet streets. There was nothing wrong with riding a bike."

"There was."

Alex said gently, "Don't be an ass, Boston."

Her lips parted, then clamped together. No one had called her "Boston" in fourteen years. He used to call her his "Boston Brahmin," which drove her up a wall. "Your language hasn't improved," she said crisply.

He shot her an amused glance. "Probably never will." Hooded eyes seared her face. "Stomach settling down?"

"There's nothing wrong with my stomach."

"I remember the cat."

So did she, the mangy tom she'd brought home and couldn't save; Alex had walked in from work and she'd had to bolt for the bathroom. Such a mortifying memory, and it was just like Alex to bring it up. "That was years ago." She suddenly couldn't swallow. "Alex. What if he . . . ?"

"No. It's not like that. We'd have heard bad news."

"You don't know that."

Alex sighed. "Is a cup of coffee going to help, or just make it worse?"

The mention of coffee was a mistake, and Alex cursed himself instantly. He should have known better. As fast as her cream complexion turned chalky, he hauled her up, shot a quick look at the appropriate sign and propelled her toward it.

The ladies' room, thankfully, was empty. Stephanie was as determined to break free of Alex's hold as she was determined not to be ill. One was possible, not the other. She twisted loose fast enough to lock herself alone in a stall and then leaned over the toilet. It was the helplessness. Jeff was in pain and she could do nothing. It was also the fear and guilt that she should have been able to do something, and there was nothing in her stomach but that terrible acid.

"Steph?"

"Would you go away? Please. I'm fine. Wonderful. Find out if anything's happened with Jeff."

But he didn't go. She straightened and leaned against the stall door. Squeezing her eyes shut, she willed the cold chills to disappear. It would have helped if *anyone* but her ex-husband had been out there.

"You're coming out of there now," he said in a don't-think-I-won't-break-down-the-door voice.

Damn the man. She flipped up the latch on the stall and walked out, head high and knees quaking. "This is the ladies' room, you know."

She was the only woman he'd ever met who would benefit from a daily shaking. Alex glared at her. He felt furious at her paleness, her pride, and her tilted-up chin when she was trembling so hard she could barely stand. He'd forgotten just how mad she could make him.

The nurse popped her head through the door, looking decidedly flustered. "The other people told me...Mrs. Carson, I'm so sorry. I had no idea you were ill." She glanced from Stephanie to Alex, registering the same surprise any stranger did when seeing them together. Patched jeans didn't usually marry with designer linen, and L'Air du Temps didn't normally hover anywhere near a grease stain. She cleared her throat, looking uncertainly at both of them. "Mrs. Carson, I can arrange transportation home for you—"

"I wouldn't suggest that, if you value your life," Alex said pleasantly.

The nurse smiled at him, certain he was making an odd little joke.

It wasn't a joke. The lass with the cap didn't know Stephanie as Alex did. She might look as delicate as her grandmother's porcelain, but she was capable of annihilating anyone who came between her and her son. The thought afforded him a moment's fleeting humor, but Stephanie was still looking like a wraith. "I'll take care of Mrs. Carson," he told the nurse.

She left a moment later. Stephanie turned her back on Alex, laid her purse on the sink and bent over to splash cool water on her face. It helped . . . at least until Alex lifted her purse and started riffling through it. His black eyes pounced on hers when he handed her the toothbrush from the bottom of her bag. "You always used to carry one."

She snatched the toothbrush and the purse, beginning to feel better again by sheer strength of will. No way she was risking being sick in front of him again. "I'm fine. You can leave now," she said crisply, and turned her face so he couldn't see while she brushed her teeth.

Alex was well aware she was irritated with him. In her world, a gentleman would have politely let her stumble to the john, let her throw up in peace and ignored her afterward. To do otherwise would have been to embarrass her—the worst of crimes in his wife's world. It was a world he'd never missed for a day, not in fourteen years. "It's not criminal, being human, Boston. When are you going to get around to learning that?"

"I wish you wouldn't call me that."

"Put on your lipstick, and stop bristling like a kitten with wet fur. I've seen you sick before. What the hell difference does it make?"

None. A lot. She didn't know. She shoved toothbrush, lipstick and brush back in her purse, then lifted her head to say something smart and snappy. But smart and snappy wouldn't come. There was something about Alex, the physical male presence of him, the steady beat in his jet-black eyes. "Alex. I want Jeff." Her voice was low and uneven, and the horrid sting of salt filled her eyes. "I want him now. I don't care about the rules. I don't care about how he looks or what's wrong—I have to see him. Please. Can't you make them . . . ?"

An old, unwanted, unfamiliar ache tugged at him. His jaw squared. "You'll see him, Boston. And right now."

The nurse urged patience. Alex, once he'd ascertained that Jeff was out of X-ray, wouldn't buy it. His first judgment, that Stephanie would be better off waiting until they'd cleaned up Jeff, was wrong. The best he could do now was make up for that.

He flanked her, going through the double doors, navigating the route to the examining room. Her step was unsteady, her eyes darting frantically around her, her body trembling when his hand reached out to steady her. And Alex marveled at her, because the moment they crossed the threshold of room seven, she changed like the flip of a switch. Her step turned sure, her eyes shone as bright as her smile and her voice was soothing as she bent down to gently kiss her son.

"This is a heck of a way to get out of doing homework," she scolded lightly. If his condition was a shock, she didn't grab him or hold on for dear life while letting a bucket of tears flow. Jeff didn't need an emotional wreck leaning over him; he needed a mother in control. And now that she could touch him, see him, hear him again, she had that control.

"You're telling me? Heck, Mom, I was afraid you'd be all worried; I kept telling them to go out and tell you I was okay. *Dad!*"

Alex leaned over to ruffle his son's hair. A cold ball was stuck in his throat. Where Stephanie had suddenly turned as solid as a brick, he could barely talk. Jeff's face was as white as the brand-new cast on his lower right leg. A long slash lined his forehead, his right eye was black and there were bloodstains on his chest. Alex never wanted to see his son in a hospital bed again. "Hurt bad?" he asked gruffly.

"Nah." Jeff grinned. "I'm tough." "Like you" was understood. "You know, I didn't do anything. I was stopped at a light, and this guy just came barreling through. The police said he was drunk, and it was in the middle of the afternoon! My bike's wrecked—"

"We'll get you a new bike," Alex promised.

Jeff's eyes glinted mischief, in spite of his pale cheeks. "A new ten-speed?"

Stephanie listened to the description of the new bike he wanted, then a blow-by-blow account of exactly how the cast had been put on. Her smile never wavered from her son. Behind her, the doctor strode in. She listened to his answers to Alex's steady battery of quiet questions: one overnight, a week off his feet, a clean break, the bruises would heal, what to do for swelling, crutches...

They stayed with him while Jeff was wheeled into a ward room with another boy. His leg was put up in traction, a TV adjusted in front of him and drinks and a Jell-Oish dinner was served. By the time the nurse brought in a shot to help Jeff sleep, Stephanie was rooted in the chair next to his bed with a mutinous glare for the woman who dared to suggest that visiting hours were over.

She held the glare at least until Alex reached for her hand and firmly locked his fingers with hers. "Okay, sport. You need your rest, and your mother could use some supper. We'll be back first thing in the morning to spring you out of here."

"I'm not leaving him," Stephanie told Alex in the hall.

"He's exhausted and he's just going to fight it the longer we stay. And two bits says you haven't had anything to eat since morning."

"He's never been alone in a hospital like this...."

"He's not six. You'll embarrass the hell out of him if you hover."

"I wasn't hovering."

Alex gave her a long look, then belatedly seemed to realize he was still holding her hand. He dropped it, and they both looked down at her slim white fingers as if startled there'd been contact. "No, you weren't," he said quietly. "I apologize. You were . . . serene. Exactly the kind of mother he needed right then."

The compliment stunned her. "It helped that you were there," she admitted.

"Where I'd like to be is anywhere within murdering distance of that drunk driver. When I first saw Jeff in that bed . . ." He dragged a hand through his hair.

"Yes." They hadn't, didn't and never would think alike about absolutely anything, but Stephanie knew they'd shared the same wrenching pain.

"He's going to be fine, Steph."

She suddenly felt oddly unnerved that Alex's reassurance meant something, that the touch of his hands had meant something in that long walk down the corridor. She had slim hands, with soft palms and well-manicured nails. They reflected the kind of life she lived. Alex's were rough, callused, blunt hands with a strong grasp that should have felt totally alien. Being touched by Alex in any way should have felt alien, wrong and out of line.

She was upset, of course. Still so upset she was barely aware darkness had fallen, that a brisk fall breeze was making her shiver and that she was being bundled into the passenger side of a pickup until the door slammed closed. Then the out-of-line sensations came full force. She hadn't been in a pickup in fourteen years. "I have my car," she told Alex when he climbed into the driver's side.

"Which I moved to the back lot when I first got here. Idiot, you left your keys in it."

"I didn't care."

"No," he said with sudden gentleness. He pushed the key in the ignition and abruptly leaned back, making no move to start the engine. Silence washed over both of them. A street lamp illuminated all the pinched lines and strained tension in Alex's face that he hadn't let his son see.

She broke the silence. "Look, it's a long drive back to Boston for you. My housekeeper will have left some kind of dinner, if you want to—"

"It's not necessary."

She stiffened. "I swear you're as stubborn as you always were...."

"I'm not stubborn."

"Fine. We'll settle for bullheaded," she said peaceably and leaned forward. "Anyway, the offer for dinner still stands...except that I'll drive my own car."

"You're not driving anywhere. Your hands are still shaking. There's no point in our driving two vehicles anyway; I can pick you up when we get Jeff in the morning. Your car can stay in the lot overnight."

She raised her purse strap to her shoulder. "Shove it, would you, Alex?" she suggested calmly.

There was a moment's silence, then Alex's husky laughter. "You may never learn to swear, Boston, but that was damn good—for you."

"My hands are not shaking, and no one pushes me around anymore."

"I wasn't trying to push you around. I figured you were sick to your stomach again—"

"I am not sick to my stomach."

"Yes, you are. Remember the cat? You must have been sick nine times—"

"Twice, maybe."

"Don't 'maybe' me. I was there." He turned on the engine and put it in gear, then lifted a brow in her direction. "Feels good to yell a little, doesn't it? Let's fight a little more. I'd almost forgotten what it feels like to have a good, loud screaming match with you—and in the meantime, you've got a little more color in your face, and I can almost convince myself I'm hungry. I don't suppose you actually stock peanut butter in that kitchen of yours."

"Peanut butter? No." She aimed a wry smile out the window. Peanut butter, beer and paper plates—that was Alex. Champagne and beef Stroganoff served on Lennox—that was her. Actually, it seemed a good night to pop open a bottle of champagne. They could celebrate the fact that Jeff really would be all right, and maybe even celebrate a divorce.

She'd never actually celebrated the end of their marriage. It belatedly occurred to her that she should have. For most people, divorces were traumatic ordeals. For her, that piece of paper was a parole from prison. She hadn't gotten over that feeling of relief in fourteen years.

"You can stop at a quick-stop for peanut butter, if you want."

"Do you have anything else edible in the house?"

"Not that you'll want."

"No surprise. Nothing changes, does it, Steph?"

There was an odd note in his voice. She turned her head to look at him. He was incredibly wrong. Everything had changed from a long time ago. Alex no longer had the power to hurt her.

Two

One couldn't escape Dartmouth in the town of Hanover, New Hampshire. The college tradition was everywhere, from the bells that rang on the half hour to the Georgian architecture to the birch trees that lined the roads. The town smelled like old money to Alex, and he'd learned the difference between old money and new when he was very young: people with old money called used furniture "antique," had lawns that looked like carpets and were embarrassed by sweat.

Driving through town, Alex felt the old chip on his shoulder he'd felt when he was seventeen, and mentally cursed himself. Truth was, as a kid he'd have sold his soul to be able to enter a school like Dartmouth.

He loved the Georgian architecture; he even loved the damn bells. Still, it was ridiculous to feel even a hint of that old gnawing inferiority. He'd succeeded without a blue-blood college and he'd made it the tough way.

Parking in front of Stephanie's driveway, he took a long look at the two-story brick house. Her father lived less than a half mile away, and she'd chosen an ivy-covered brick building like the house she'd grown up in, with polished casement windows and mammoth shrubs lining the walk to the door. Alex allowed himself one immature moment of gut pleasure, thinking that he could buy a half dozen houses like this for her now, and then mentally chided himself again. Foolish, that it still mattered. And he still couldn't stop himself from pushing off his work boots the minute he entered the door.

Stephanie, hurrying ahead of him to turn on lights, paused at the kitchen doorway with an uncertain smile. "You don't have to take off your shoes, Alex...."

No? Her living-room carpet was cream—not virgin white, but close. Both her couches were velvet, and that same unmarred, dauntingly feminine cream. Lime and pink pillows were arranged just so. Royal Doulton figures sat gracefully on tables, and an oil painting of her father over the marble mantel glared at him, as if daring Alex to put a grease stain anywhere near his daughter's domain.

He bent his head to the grocery bag he was carry-
ing. No peanut butter. He wasn't *that* obsessed with it.
But thank God he'd bought beer because he suddenly
needed one. At the hospital, he hadn't been inclined
to strand his ex-wife in a dark house alone to worry all
night about their son. Now that he was here he knew
just how ridiculous a thought that was. Stephanie
didn't need him. She'd never needed him. And being
in her house was enough to raise a few memories he
could do completely without.

"I'll get you a glass."

"Don't bother. I'll drink from the can."

Stephanie nodded. Alex's tone was crisp and distant, and his smile had disappeared the minute he entered the house. She suddenly felt off balance,
although there wasn't a reason on earth they had to be
chattily pleasant with each other. It was enough that
he was here. Jeff's absence shouted from every corner like a lonely echo. And as for Alex, she had no
reason to feel uncomfortable.

She flicked on a light switch in the kitchen. The
small brass chandelier blinked on, shining softly on
the polished oak table. She moved the dried flower
centerpiece and set out cloth place mats, mentally as-
suring herself that she was behaving naturally. "Myrt
left more than enough dinner." She opened the refrigerator. "Beef Stroganoff. All I have to do is re-
heat it in the microwave."

"I'll do it. You sit down."

"I can..." His arm brushed her hip, and she moved away quickly. Silence settled like an uncomfortable cloud on a too-humid day. Alex took out silverware. He knew where it was. It wasn't as if he'd never been in the kitchen before. He'd just always been here when Jeff was around at the same time. She took out dinner plates. Heavens, that made a lot of noise.

Suddenly there wasn't any noise at all but the hum of the microwave. And the two "strangers" stared at each other.

Stephanie cleared her throat. "Your business must be doing well if you've expanded to Boston. Jeff's always talking about your cars."

He shot her an amused glance. "You don't want to hear about antique cars." He reached in the refrigerator, found a barely opened bottle of wine and started searching for a wineglass. "Jeff says you're getting quite a name as an appraiser these days. Working Vermont and New Hampshire with that company of yours?"

She said dryly, "You want to hear about the business of appraising estates about as much as I want to hear about antique cars, Alex."

"I wouldn't mind."

She shook her head. "It would bore you to bits, and you know it." She glanced with surprise at the glass she seemed to have accepted. "I really don't need a drink."

"You have to." A flash of humor in his eyes, he motioned gravely to his beer. "I never drink alone."

"Well, in that case..." She smiled, sipping the wine, but she found herself staring at him and became furious with herself for being so awkward. Alex had picked up Jeff a thousand times over the years. He was no stranger, and the old wounds had healed over time. There was no excuse for this nervousness.

But Alex hadn't been alone with her in all that time, and she now found herself seeing him in a different way. She had no idea what he did with his time to keep his skin so sun-burnished gold. And when had he earned that furrow between his brows that she'd never noticed before? She really didn't know him, not anymore.

The thing was, Stephanie mused, a woman meeting Alex for the first time would see him differently than she did. A woman first meeting him, for instance, might notice that his forearms and thighs were like steel, and that he moved quietly, in the way of a man who concealed his power. And a woman meeting him the first time might make the disastrous assumption that Alex was a gentle man, simply because he had a gentle mouth.

His lips *were* soft. It was the twist of his smile that was dangerous. She scanned his features, from the strong bones to the straight nose, to the square chin, and paused absently on his eyes. Skip the smile, actually. His eyes were the real hazard for an unsuspecting woman. At first glance, they were simply brown, except that "simply brown" implied a puppy dog docility and Alex's had none of that quality. His eyes could sear right through a woman, strip off the civilized layers with ruthless speed and then suddenly turn infinitely compassionate and tender.

Alex, Stephanie concluded absently, was a dangerously sexy man. Which she'd always known. She'd just forgotten. She took a long sip of wine, her reward for being completely immune to his charms.

The microwave pinged and they both jumped for it. Stephanie was diverted when the phone rang. Minutes later, Alex set her plate next to the counter by the phone, but she didn't have the chance to eat. George called first, wanting to know what had happened with Jeff. He wasn't happy that she was planning to take the next week off.

She'd no sooner hung up than her housekeeper called. Myrt, too, had to be informed that with Stephanie home for a week, her services wouldn't be needed. After that, she had to call one of Jeff's teachers to let him know what had happened. Then her father phoned. Everyone asked for a full range of details. She gave them, rubbing her temples with two fingers as a few minutes gradually dragged into a half hour. Lord, she was tired!

She'd barely sat down and lifted a fork before the phone jangled again. One of Jeff's friends.... She handled it. And when it rang yet again, Alex firmly grabbed the phone, answered it himself and, when he was through, set the phone off the hook and grabbed her plate to rewarm it in the microwave.

An hour ago he hadn't known what he was doing in her house. Now he did. For a few minutes she'd had color in her face. Now it was gone again. She never used common sense. It was so important for her to be polite to other people even when she was totally exhausted, and the last thing she needed was to relive Jeff's accident over and over. The infuriating woman needed a keeper.

Stephanie shook her head when he handed her the rewarmed plate. "I couldn't."

"Just a bite."

"Alex—"

"And a little more wine." He poured it, then settled back in the chair across from her, loosely crossing his arms on the table.

"All right," she agreed, because it was easier than saying nothing, but after that she felt permanently on stall. What on earth could they talk about?

"Tough, isn't it?" Alex murmured.

She looked up.

"Maybe it would be easier if we started from scratch. Hello, I'm Alex Carson, your ex-husband. I work out of New York and Boston and I restore antique cars. I have a helluva big family."

Stephanie chuckled, feeling more at ease. At least he was having the same problem she was. "How's your mom and dad?"

"Ornery as usual. I figure they're going to get a divorce when they're both about eighty. That's the soonest they'll ever get around to agreeing on grounds—or anything else.''

"Alex! They're happily married!"

"They fight all the time."

"They've always fought all the time. They love to fight.''

"True." Alex unobtrusively ladled a second helping on her plate. His ex-wife was eating like a starving street waif, but he didn't dare mention it. She wouldn't appreciate the image, and the renewed sparkle in her eyes was enough reward. "You know, you've been living in this house two years now, but you never did tell me why you moved from your father's place. I figured you were installed there for life."

"Oh, well..." Will Randolph was usually a subject best avoided anywhere near Alex. "I wanted a place of my own," she said simply. "Jeff was getting to an age where the music was getting too loud. Dad was getting to an age where he was getting fussier about quietness. Before we had any problems, I just felt..."

He nodded, and spooned a little more onto her plate. "Jeff says you've been seeing some guy for a while now."

She set down her fork. "Alex, I didn't move because of some man, if that's what you're thinking. If you think I would do anything immoral around Jeff, particularly at his sensitive age—"

"I wasn't criticizing—or prying," Alex said soothingly. "Just making conversation, Boston. You're entitled to your private life. And Jeff had been talking about this guy...."

"Jeff has a terror I'm going to marry anyone I date twice," Stephanie said wryly, and picked up her fork again. The sound of "Boston" this time made her toes curl. Or maybe it was the wine making her toes curl. She was too tired to feel defensive, and glanced up with surprise when Alex stole the empty plate from in front of her. She surely hadn't eaten the whole thing. "Alex? Do you think he's sleeping all right?"

"I think he's probably sleeping like a rock." Alex knew immediately she was talking about their son.

"You don't think he'll wake up in pain?"

"He'll have a shot if he does, Boston. But nature's pretty good about broken bones. Generally shock sets in, and the limb feels more numb than painful for a day or so."

"How do you know that?" Stephanie stood up to rinse her plate and set it in the dishwasher.

"I've broken limbs, one arm and one leg."

"You never told me that before," she said with surprise.

"I never told you about trying to shave fuzz off a peach with my father's electric razor when I was seven, either. Want to know what my dad had to say at the time?"

"No," Stephanie said wryly, "I *know* what your father had to say, and it was all four-letter words." Alex chuckled behind her, and she snatched a dishrag for the counters. "Want me to do your shirt?" she asked casually.

"Pardon?"

"It wouldn't be anything to throw it in the washer. I was thinking..." She hesitated, then turned around to face him as she wiped her hands on a towel. "You have to be as tired as I am, and it's a darn long drive all the way back to Boston, only to turn around first thing in the morning for Jeff. Not that you have to be there to pick him up with me—"

"I told Jeff I'd be there, and I will."

"Yes." Alex wouldn't break a promise if he had a date with a coffin. Stephanie never doubted that. "So there's three bedrooms upstairs. You could sleep in Jeff's or the spare one. And assuming you wanted a clean shirt in the morning..."

"I wouldn't put you out, staying here?"

"You wouldn't be putting me out. I'm going to bed, and you can do as you please. I was just offering." She couldn't not offer. Bleak lines of exhaustion lined his eyes. He was dead tired, he was the father of her son, and she was hardly going to treat him like an enemy. Fourteen years of being divorced had proved that Alex posed no threat to her, and to offer him a bed for the night simply seemed the civilized thing to do. She refused to think there was anything strange about it.

"All right. If you're sure—"

"I'm sure, and if you want me to do your shirt..."

"I can manage a washing machine by myself." He was already starting to take the shirt off.

Five buttons later he tugged it off his shoulders and strode to the laundry room just off her kitchen. Stephanie stood, unmoving, her eyes unwillingly riveted to him. His shoulders and arms were a ripple of muscle, his chest solid as rock. It wasn't weight-lifting sinew, not the shape of a man who occasionally exercised to keep fit, but the shape of a man who physically worked long and hard for a living, day after day. Rock would have been softer. Even the crisp black hair on his chest was springy. In fact, she could remember the exact texture of that hair, the feel of her hands curled in it, the feel of her breasts crushed against him.

Alex flopped down the top of the washer and stepped back into the kitchen. Dark eyes suddenly met blue. The current between them was swift, sharp and totally unexpected. She found her voice. "If you think you can manage, I'll just go up to bed then."

"Fine. Sleep well—and thanks for the offer of a bed."

"No problem."

But she had a problem sleeping. The hours ticked off on her bedside clock, one after the other. The night was dark and cloudy. A fall wind whipped leaves against the windows. She heard when Alex came upstairs, heard him quietly shut the far door to the spare bedroom.

She closed her eyes. Everything was right to relax her. The sheets were cool and soft, her nightgown slinky against her bare skin, her pillow fluffed and refluffed. Her bedroom was filled with comfortably familiar things—the small white velvet love seat in the corner, her favorite vials of perfume on the dresser, her collection of alabaster and porcelain boxes on the table by the window. She tried to think about boxes, and instead couldn't stop thinking about Alex.

She was *not* relaxed.

At 3:00 A.M. she gave up, reached for the long white robe at the bottom of the bed and tiptoed with infinite care down the stairs. Alex—at least he used to— would wake up at the drop of a pin. She didn't even consider putting on a light as she wandered past the living room and into the den.

The den was Jeff's lair. He'd picked out the overstuffed rust sofa and put up the brick and board bookshelves the year before. He needed a place to crash in his grubbies, he'd told her, and she hadn't objected. She dropped into the corner of the couch and drew her knees up.

"Couldn't sleep, either?"

She nearly jumped out of her skin. "Alex! I didn't see you!"

And she still didn't, beyond the vague shadow in the chair in the far corner of the room. "Would wine help?"

She hesitated. "Please."

He returned from the kitchen a moment later. Their fingers touched when he handed her the wine, and she took a quick sip, disturbed with the small contact, irritated with herself because of it. She was glad he hadn't turned on a light. As her eyes became accustomed to the dark, she could see he was dressed as she'd left him, in jeans and nothing else. She took another quick sip of wine. "I couldn't stop thinking about Jeff," she murmured.

"I couldn't stop thinking about you." Alex's tone was both soft and blunt. He leaned his head back in the chair, aware he'd startled her. He was also aware that she couldn't see him well, while he could see her perfectly. Her pale profile showed up against the dark couch. Silky strands of champagne hair tumbled down her back. That color almost couldn't be natural, but he knew it was. She was elegant even at three in the morning. The silk robe was draped lovingly over her body; the fragile scent of her perfume whispered toward him in the darkness.

He should have known there wasn't a prayer in hell he could sleep in this house. "I was thinking what damn fools we were at seventeen."

For a moment she tensed, wary of remembering, but the tension faded like a surprise. It really was a long time ago. "There could hardly have been worse ones," she agreed.

"I was remembering the wedding. Or more exactly, the car breaking down between the justice of the peace and the motel."

She chuckled. "That old jalopy—and I nearly killed you. You were under the car and you told me to put it in neutral and I put it in drive."

"You *did* run over my foot."

"Good Lord. Are you still holding a grudge?"

"A little."

"Well, to heck with you. *I* still remember what you said about the first roast I made."

"Boston. A dog couldn't have eaten that roast."

"You could have at least *tried*."

"I might have, but by then you'd thrown it at me. Including the carrots."

The wine was gliding down her throat like honey. "I always had the impression," she said gravely, "that you resented the carrots most."

"I did. Next to the time I had the guys over for poker, and you served them little cucumber sandwiches cut up in triangles."

"I was trying to be a hostess. How was I supposed to know they wanted beer and potato chips?"

"Was that any reason to lock me out of the house?"

"You deserved it," Stephanie assured him.

"It was colder than hell frozen over that night!"

"I'm the one who suffered. I had to nurse you through a cold. Judging from the way you acted, I thought you were dying."

"I would have rather died the day your father made an unexpected call, and found me chasing you around the house stark naked."

A slight jolt rocked through her system. That wasn't nice of Alex, bringing up the more intimate memories. On the other hand, no one would ever accuse Alex of being nice, and Stephanie didn't fold up these days under a little adversity. "That was just as embarrassing for me as for you," she pointed out calmly. "I wasn't wearing anything, either."

Alex reached up and switched on a lamp.

Stephanie blinked at the sudden light. "What'd you do that for?"

"I was looking for your blush, Boston."

"That," she informed him, "isn't fair."

"You used to blush all the time." His grin was wickedly mischievous. "Heck, Steph, way back when, I thought you were going to live locked in the bathroom. God forbid I should see you brushing your teeth. Lightning might strike if I saw you with a curler in your hair—"

"Darnit, Alex, I was seventeen and feeling awkward and you were male. You grew up in a house where all kinds of things were natural that weren't in mine. I didn't know how to be natural around you."

"That wasn't the problem," he said gravely.

"Then what was?"

"You were monopolizing the only john in the apartment," he reminded her dryly.

She laughed, throwing back her head. "Listen, Carson, you were as sensitive about personal things as I was."

"Name one," he said disbelievingly.

"Fine. You were fooling around with a wrench one day and the thing dropped, and the next thing I know you're doubled over."

"You don't need to bring up that one."

"And you're groaning, 'I'm fine I'm fine but don't count on any more children after this.' Good Lord, I thought you were dying. All you had to do was tell me...."

"There are some things a seventeen-year-old boy doesn't know how to tell a lady."

"I see the old double standard is alive and well," she said dryly, and finished her wine. The cool, sweet liquid slid down her throat, warming her stomach. How strange to be able to laugh about it all. None of it had been funny at the time. She murmured, "You think we were just a little guilty of taking ourselves too seriously?"

"There was more than that," he said quietly.

She knew. Her eyes met his through the darkness. They both knew.

Getting married at seventeen was insane for anyone, and they'd had additional strikes against them. Small things, like her father chasing after them and having Alex arrested for statutory rape. Tiny problems, like a girl raised with maid service suddenly stranded in a one-room apartment over a garage with a checkbook that only bounced if she wrote checks. Little things, like his parents disliking her. Like a pregnancy.

Those things were bad enough, but they weren't what split them apart. Alex knew. She could see the old pain in his eyes, could feel the old ache inside of her. And she didn't want it. Not now, not ever. Pain was an emotion that took too damn much energy, and she'd wasted enough of that a long time ago. She stood up. "I think," she murmured, "I'm finally tired."

"And I'm right behind you."

He switched out the light, and trailed her up the stairs in the darkness. She felt suddenly angry, wishing she'd never asked him to stay, yet glad she had. The old accusations—she didn't need to be reminded of them again. Yet it had felt special to laugh with Alex, and on this night she hadn't wanted to be alone, with no one who could possibly understand that but the father of her son. At the door to her room, she paused. "Thank you," she said quietly.

"For what?"

"For being there with me this afternoon, with Jeff. You've always been a good father to him. If I never said that to you before..."

It piled up very suddenly. The look of Jeff in the hospital bed—all battered—the waiting, the wretched drive and feeling sick, and standing on her head to make Jeff smile when all she'd wanted to do was cry.

Alex's arm closed around her, his callused hand pushing the hair back from her face. His thumb gently rubbed the moisture on her cheeks. Damn tears. She hadn't cried in years. A Randolph didn't cry. A Randolph was raised never to cry, to have total control over one's emotions at all time. A Randolph was raised New England strong. Staunch. Stiff upper lip.

Her upper lip was quivering.

He leaned against the wall, drawing her to him. Lifting her face with his finger on her chin, he smoothed away more of the tears on her cheeks with the pad of his callused thumb. "You know, you wouldn't get sick to your stomach if you'd cry when you needed to. You always did keep it all in."

"Oh, shut up. I don't want to cry."

"It's good for you," Alex coaxed.

"It isn't. It's . . . ugly."

"Boston. Try not to talk irrational nonsense."

"I'm not irrational. I'm a calm, rational, sensible woman and I *hate* crying." And the very good reason she'd never been alone with him before in fourteen years was that Alex always made her say ridiculous things.

"Here." He dug a handkerchief from his jeans pocket. "Blow."

"No."

He held the handkerchief over her nose until she did. A foghorn was not a glamorous sound.

"Can you breathe now?" The handkerchief went back into his pocket.

"Yes," she said crossly.

"Good. Because I'm going to kiss you."

She ducked, fast.

Alex was faster, his mouth capturing her swiftly, his warmth surrounding her like a surprise. Nasty sensations tiptoed into her consciousness. Desire, loneliness, an echo of something terribly powerful. Her heart suddenly felt trapped in her chest.

She stood absolutely rigid, her palms against the wall, the pulse in her throat throbbing. She'd so completely forgotten that there was another definite problem with finding herself alone with Alex. He kissed like the devil.

For fourteen years, of course, he had been kissing other women. Undoubtedly so many that perhaps he'd become confused. In the morning Alex was going to be darned embarrassed, and for right now she was going to do him a favor and respond like a piece of petrified wood.

His mouth pressed, then teased on hers, smooth and warm. His tongue flicked out and dampened her lips. That tongue was hot. And slow. And the fingers of his one hand stole in her hair, the pressure of his palm lifting her face for him. She could have made a fuss, but she was busy showing him that she was unaffected.

Again, his lips leveled on hers. This time he took a step closer, the step necessary to obliterate the distance from thigh to thigh, breast to chest. Silk and denim rustled together. He tasted like Alex. Stephanie had made a major effort in the intervening years to kiss a lot of men; none of them tasted like Alex. All right, dammit, she still felt it. Thirty-one years old, and she still hadn't gotten over this irresponsible craving for the man. What did that prove? Lust wasn't worth horseradish.

Someone was sliding his fingers through the satin loop at the top of her robe. He was watching her, his eyes lighting up the darkness with black silver. And then he wasn't watching her, because his eyes closed when he bent his head to hers again. He claimed her mouth and with the same lazy assurance he claimed her silk-clad breast.

Just once, she'd like to be touched by him when her heart wasn't pounding. Her hands slipped up his arms, onto his shoulders, needing to hold on to something. His skin was sleek and warm, cloaking the power of muscle beneath it. It wasn't entirely her fault for giving in. It was his, for making her feel small, crushable, infinitely feminine. Any woman could get lost in this man.

At seventeen, he'd always been in such a hurry. Nothing had changed. No slow flames for Alex; he still liked forest fires. He was greedy and hungry, and his lips were lonely, desperately lonely.

So was she. Oh God, so was she. All her life, the whole world had treated her like spun cotton, but never Alex. Alex was cruel, demanding things of her no one had ever demanded, and taking them. Only he never had enough....

And neither did she. Her fingers combed through his hair, and she swayed against him, the tips of her silk-clad nipples grazing his bare flesh. An earthy hiss left his throat, affording her enormous satisfaction. His mouth left hers, trailed the line of her jaw and ducked down to the hollow below her collarbone. He knew she couldn't stand that. He had no right to remember that that spot was vulnerable.

The lower part of Alex's body molded against hers, jeans to silk, his arousal to the softest part of her belly.

Wanting spread through her in a lush, warm flood. She felt silky with it, crazy with it, light-headed and...abruptly startled when Alex suddenly jerked back from her. He was breathing hard, and his eyes were as shiny as a lake at midnight.

"When the hell were you going to get around to stopping me?" he rasped.

She felt suddenly helpless as a kitten in a rainstorm, and furious at the same time. "Why the hell did you start it?"

His hand touched her cheek; his lips twisted. "You just swore."

"I did not."

"You did. And I started it because I want you. The same way, and to the same extent, that I've always wanted you. Only you weren't supposed to want me back. Boston, this is a hell of a state of affairs." He pushed the half-open door to her bedroom until it swung wide. "Lock it," he said roughly, and strode down the hall.

Three

————

At quarter to six in the morning Stephanie heard the doorknob to her bedroom turn. It was still dark, that hazy predawn charcoal before the sun comes up. Through half-closed eyes she saw Alex walk toward the bed on bare feet and then hesitate. She didn't move, didn't so much as breathe. After a few minutes, he leaned over and planted two fists on the mattress next to her.

"You always were the worst faker who ever lived, Steph. Neither of us is sleeping. I'll make the coffee."

It took her twenty minutes to don camel slacks and a soft topaz sweater, sweep her hair in a neat coil and apply an adequate amount of makeup to cover the smudges of a sleepless night under her eyes. When she entered the kitchen, her expression was as remote and controlled as a winning gambler in a poker game.

Two frying pans were on the stove. Alex had a fork in one hand and a spatula in the other, one turning bacon and the other ready to flip the eggs. His feet were bare, his clean shirt untucked and loose over his jeans, and his night beard hadn't seen a razor yet. Stephanie could have stepped back in time to mornings a long time ago. Alex was invariably casual to her meticulous neat, shaggy to her trimmed, and strikingly dominantly male to her female. He glanced up. There was a steady beat in his dark eyes when he looked at her. A disturbing beat.

Her fingers leaped for the cameo at her throat. Alex's eyes immediately jumped there. A tactical error in dressing, that cameo. She always wore it when she needed a charm to get her through a day, but who could have guessed he'd remember after all this time? She hurried toward the refrigerator. "I've got honeydew melon, if you'd like. And toast.... I would think we could pick up Jeff fairly early from the hospital, don't you?"

She set the table with her mother's Lennox china and sterling-silver utensils, started the coffee, sliced the melon and buried the toast in thick guava jelly. By the time Alex served the eggs and bacon, a pale sun was peeking in the windows and the table looked as if it held a feast for ten. Stephanie picked up her fork and wondered how she was going to swallow any of it.

"Stop it, Stephanie."

She looked up with her best civilized smile. "Stop what?"

Alex leaned back in his chair and rubbed the ache at his nape with an impatient hand. Irritation mixed with amusement glinted in his dark eyes. Stephanie was the only woman he knew who served orange juice in crystal, came to breakfast wearing lipstick and could lie—albeit badly—with a smile. "You can relax," he said dryly. "It's not going to happen again."

The faintest warmth colored her cheeks. "Of course, it isn't," she agreed instantly. Her voice came out in a rush, echoing every word she'd prepared in the hours she was trying so hard to sleep. "For heaven's sake, Alex, I wasn't going to make anything of it. You had a beer, I had some wine. We were both exhausted, both emotionally strung out over Jeff—"

"So relax," Alex interrupted.

"I am relaxed." And getting irritated, she thought.

"Then take your hand off that cameo and dig in," Alex suggested. "And you don't have to fake all the politeness around me, Boston. You're entitled to do a little ranting and raving if you want to. I was way out of line."

She had no desire to rant and rave but considered, briefly, pouring a cup of coffee over his head. She didn't, of course, because she was a woman who took pride in keeping her feelings under control. If she hadn't kept a firm handle on her emotions, she might easily have murdered Alex on any number of occasions over the years. The man was somehow the most arrogant when his voice was the most soothing. He had the irritating habit of pouncing on the truth when a white lie would have been a thousand times more comfortable. And she felt a ridiculous blend of relief, hurt, rage and distress that he was so lazily dismissing the night before.

He *had* been way out of line. She was not going to forget it. All she wanted to forget was the way she'd melted like Silly Putty in his arms.

She picked up her fork again and swallowed a bite of eggs. "Delicious, Alex," she commented brightly.

He just looked at her.

The day had to get better once they picked up Jeff.

"Mom! Dad! I didn't think you were ever going to get here!"

Since it was only eight o'clock in the morning the comment was hardly fair, but one look at Jeff, and Stephanie wished they'd arrived sooner. True, her son was wearing a grin, but his bruises were twice as colorful as yesterday. She hadn't seen bandages on his chest the day before, and the white cast on his lower leg looked a dozen times bigger than she'd remembered it. She wanted him home, where she could mother him to absolute death.

"Did you sleep okay?" She couldn't stop herself from pushing back the straggly lock of hair from his forehead. He grimaced at the maternal gesture.

"Sure, I slept okay, except they woke us up practically at dawn to give us breakfast. Let's get out of here. The doctor's already been in; he says I'm fine."

"I know. We talked to him. You have to keep that leg up for at least a couple days, Jeff—"

"Sure. Which jeans did you bring?"

"Not your favorites, but don't give me a hard time. We'll have to cut these to get around the cast, don't forget—"

"Yeah, I know." Jeff looked first at his mother, then his father, and beamed. "Sure is nice to have us all together," he mentioned. "Just like a regular family, you know?"

Stephanie froze. Alex stepped forward. "Your mother's going to get you checked out while I help you get dressed, sport. We'll have you out of here within a half hour."

It took a little longer than that. Checking him out took only minutes, but Jeff wasn't as strong as he was determined to be and using crutches wasn't as easy as he'd expected. Stephanie wanted him to use a wheelchair, and was treated to a scowl.

"Mom, stop fussing."

"Hey. Your mother's worried to death about you, and if she wants you to use a wheelchair getting out of here..."

"Sure, Dad. Sorry, Mom."

She treated Alex to an irritated frown. If her son wanted to be testy, he could be testy. Heaven knew, no male could be as difficult as Alex when he was ill.

Jeff used the wheelchair without another word until they passed through the hospital doors. Minutes later, he was settled by the passenger window of Alex's truck, and his grin was back in place as they started toward home. He leaned forward so he could look at both of them. His grin suddenly became wider. "So what'd you two do last night?" he asked conversationally. "Dad, did you take Mom out to dinner?"

"No, we ate at your house." Alex flicked on a turn signal, studied a lot of traffic that wasn't there and turned left onto Park St. Stephanie's very shapely thigh was pressed against his. It was an extremely tense thigh, and the faint tease of her perfume whispered around him.

"Well, did you guys do anything afterward? Like take in a movie or something?"

"We were fairly tired, Jeff."

"Well, you didn't drive all the way back to Boston, did you? Mom, didn't you tell him to stay the night?"

Stephanie fussed with the cameo at her throat, and looked calm. It wasn't easy to look relaxed when she was suffering from shock. How long had Jeff been harboring hope that the two of them would get back together? How fast could she get rid of Alex and have a quick, potent, effective talk with her son? "This afternoon, there's a teacher coming from school to bring you your schoolwork."

"Aw, Mom."

"You've had approximately four hundred calls from your friends just since yesterday. Barry, John,

Checkers, Nate, Julie—*who* is Julie?—and I told them all they could visit, as of tomorrow, and only for short spurts after school.''

"Not today? The bruises will probably be all healed by tomorrow."

A thought that depressed the son; the mother only wished it were true. "Myrt won't be here this week, but I will, Jeff. I'll make your favorite things to eat. I figured we'd get out the old Monopoly board, and you told me I had to learn that computer game.... What's the name?''

"Ghostbusters. Dad, you're going to stick around a little, too, aren't you? We can do a whole bunch of things together." Jeff added delicately, "Not that you both have to be around me the whole time. It's not as if I'm sick. You guys can go out to dinner and stuff like that."

At the house, Stephanie murmured one hissed "What is this?" to Alex, but then the next hour was a flurry of activity. Before they'd gone to the hospital, she'd fixed up the den as a sick room—but Jeff wanted to be set up in his bedroom, close to his books and stereo and computer. Alex moved in a TV. Stephanie hurried to bring in a table within reach of his bed. The whole time Jeff grinned at both of them, like a benevolent genie pleased with his magical efforts to make the two work together as a team.

"This is just great, just great." Jeff beamed. "You two used to argue a lot when I was a kid, right? Not anymore. Nobody's arguing about anything, did you notice? Everybody's real happy—''

"Your mother," Alex interrupted abruptly, "is going downstairs to get herself a cup of coffee."

Stephanie fled. Alex sat down heavily at the edge of the bed.

"Did you get a chance to talk to Mom about a dog?"

"No."

"The basketball net?"

"Sport," Alex said firmly, "you and I are the ones who need a little talk, not me and your mother."

Stephanie took an aspirin for her pounding head, spent fifteen minutes dithering, glanced at the clock and decided it was a reasonable hour to prepare a lunch tray for Jeff. She set out the sterling silver tray. She didn't think he'd want anything too heavy, and settled on crisp lettuce with delicate slices of cheese— what exactly was Alex saying to him up there?—then cut the sandwiches in diamonds and sliced off the crusts. As a little boy Jeff had always loved fancy little sandwiches.

She found some small blue cocktail napkins that matched the blue painted flowers on the china, added a wedge of lemon in the chilled glass of iced tea and, as an afterthought, added a small bud vase. When she was done, the tray would surely have tempted a monk on a fast, and she headed up the stairs feeling momentarily more like herself. So the night before she'd nearly been seduced on the hall floor by an ex-husband who'd never once let on he wanted her in all these years. So this morning she discovered her fourteen-year-old son had been blithely imagining reconciliations. She'd cope with all that later. She was a mother first and foremost today and, darn it, she'd always been a good one.

Alex was hunched over in a chair by the bed, dealing cards. They were playing poker, using toothpicks for antes. Stephanie took one look and felt a falling sensation. Both heads looked alike, both full of thick rich, brown hair with the same cowlick in back, both heads finger-combed in evident dead-serious concentration. Whatever talk they'd had had ended quickly and obviously well. Stephanie had never clashed with Jeff until he reached puberty. Now it seemed father and son naturally belonged together. The smallest example was that she'd never once considered playing poker with Jeff. She didn't even know how.

"Lunchtime," she said brightly.

"Great. I'm starved!" Jeff pushed aside the cards and accepted the tray on his lap. He took one look and then glanced at his dad.

Stephanie abruptly wished she could have drowned in the bud vase, and knew at an instant she shouldn't have cut up the sandwiches. Jeff wasn't a child anymore. She had to try harder to remember that. The problem was that ever since he'd turned fourteen there were days when he behaved like an errant nine-year-old and days when he behaved like a man. A soothsayer couldn't have told which mood he'd wake up in, but that didn't make her feel any better at the moment.

"Looks great, doesn't it, Jeff?" Alex prodded.

"Great. Just great." Jeff beamed at Stephanie.

"If you want something else, honey... I felt you didn't need anything heavy on your stomach, but if you're really hungry—"

"No, this is fine. Just what I was hoping you'd make."

"I knew the flower was silly. I just put it on there to make you laugh."

"Mom, it looks great."

"Well, good." She fingered the cameo at her throat, and looked at a spot directly to the left of Alex's eyes. "If you'd like me to make you some lunch, too..."

"No need. I just told Jeff I was going to take off for a few hours. I need a chance to change clothes and make some arrangements at the shop—"

"He'll be back tonight, Mom. That's okay, isn't it?" Careful tact reeked from Jeff's tone, something he'd obviously been coached to learn very quickly.

"Of course it's okay. Whatever you and your father want is fine by me." She'd just have to find time to stock the house with more aspirin beforehand.

Alex stood up and a slash of lightning crackled in the room. It was nothing anyone could see, just something that happened when his arm brushed against hers. Guilt followed, like the scolding of a toddler who'd stolen a cookie. *Nonono Stephanie.*

When it rained, it really poured. Alex might or might not have accidentally touched her through the years; she'd never noticed. Now, since last night, the slightest pressure of his fingers on her nape evoked free-form sexual fantasies, all as delicious as they were taboo. What exactly have I done to deserve this? she thought glumly.

As Alex said a quick goodbye to Jeff, his palm gently increased the pressure on her arm, and she belatedly understood that he wanted her to accompany him to the hallway. When she followed him a short distance from Jeff's room, he placed both hands on her shoulders. Obviously there was something terribly wrong with her entire head today, because she could have sworn his eyes held an intense, intimate, male glow when they looked at her.

And his tone was ridiculously gentle. "If it's going to make you uncomfortable, I won't come back tonight."

"Of course it won't make me uncomfortable."

"I'll probably stay at the Inn a few times this week. If I can accomplish a fair amount of business this afternoon, I can clear away some solid time for Jeff. Free you up a little."

"I don't need to be 'freed up,' but you can spend as much time with Jeff as you want. You know that, Alex. He loves time with you."

"Do you want me to take care of getting your car from the hospital lot?"

She'd forgotten all about it. "I can."

"I'll handle it."

She nodded. He could do anything he wanted as long as he took his hands off her shoulders. Soon. To move away seemed childish. Alex was only standing close to ensure that Jeff didn't hear. Regardless, it wasn't his fault little shivers were chasing up and down her spine.

All this time she'd been immune. Knowing there was attraction wasn't what unnerved her. Strangers could feel attraction, but strangers didn't give in to it as she had last night. She felt vulnerable and didn't like it. She wasn't supposed to be vulnerable with Alex anymore.

"Boston?"

"Hmm?" She thought it would be easier to look at his mouth than his eyes. Wrong. She stared at his mouth and remembered the first time they made love in a '53 MG, the kind with the running boards and the long sleek hood. It hadn't been easy to make love between the leather bucket seats and a shift on the floor. Logistics should have made it impossible. But those same devilish eyes had made her do it, that same coaxing mouth. When desire was that strong, unfortunately anything was possible and nothing so minor as morals or awkward bucket seats made any difference.

"Could I have your attention?"

Stephanie felt reality zip up her errant imagination. "You've had my total attention."

"Good," Alex murmured absently. He would have paid a fortune to figure out what put the misty look in her soft eyes. Damn woman. He was as aroused as a teenage boy just looking at her. The problem was that he wanted to do a lot more than look. "I just wanted to tell you that I had nothing to do with it. With Jeff, and his sudden little hints that he wants the two of us together."

"I never said you did."

"I'm sure you felt awkward—"

"I didn't feel the least awkward," she lied blithely. "He's just of an awkward age...but it did occur to me that one of us should have taught our son a little more tact."

"I talked to him."

"Good. We can't have him thinking foolish things like that. I read somewhere that most kids of divorced homes secretly wish the parents would get back together, but in our case, that's ridiculous...."

"It certainly is." He dropped his hands from her shoulders; she felt the breath rush from her lungs, and he was climbing down the stairs a moment later. With a sigh she returned to Jeff's room and settled in the chair next to his bed while he finished his lunch. Midday sun was pouring through the windows, throwing light on the conglomerate psychedelic posters on the wall. Jeff had chosen his own decor, and as far as Stephanie could tell it was early electric cord. The phone, computer, stereo and radio he called a "box" all had cords. For about a year, she'd worried that her son would go into a decline if the power went out. One of the last arguments she'd had with Alex—discussions, she corrected herself—was over her spoiling of Jeff.

It had bothered her for months and still did. She really didn't want to spoil Jeff. A spoiled boy made for a spoiled man. She did want him to have the best of everything, exposure to all the arts, all the different kinds of music, every educational tool she could afford for him. Life was tough, and all she could do as a parent was give him the best start she knew how. That wasn't spoiling him, was it?

Why did she suddenly feel unsure of herself as a mother? She lifted the tray from Jeff's lap when he was done, and noticed the deck of cards on the table. She stared at them for a moment. "Want to teach me poker?"

Jeff's brows lifted in surprise, but he leaned over with all enthusiasm and rattled off the values of different sets of cards so fast she could barely follow. "Now, if you're going to play this right, you have to try hard not to think like a girl, Mom."

"I'll try."

"I mean some girls think more like girls than others. You always think like a girl, if you know what I mean."

She had no idea what he meant, and was afraid to ask.

"Bets." Her son looked as if he belonged in a casino, wearing a satin vest.

"One toothpick."

"That's a girl's bet, Mom."

"Four toothpicks."

"That's better."

A few minutes later she laid down four threes and waited expectantly. Jeff stared at her cards and then at her. "You're getting no more coaching," he said heavily.

"You had three kings. I only had threes."

He shook his head in despair. "I think this game is beyond you. Maybe we'll try cribbage."

They tried cribbage for an hour, until Stephanie could see that Jeff was getting tired. She put away the cards and dropped the shades at the windows, as ready for a nap as her son.

"Mom?" Jeff called when she reached the doorway.

She turned with a smile.

"Dad said I embarrassed you. Like . . . I'm sorry."

A fierce wave of love rushed through her. "Nothing you could do or say would ever embarrass me, honey. Nothing to be sorry about." She hesitated and knew that wasn't quite enough to say. "Jeff, your father and I aren't enemies. It wasn't that kind of divorce. I'm delighted he's going to be around here to spend time with you this week, for your sake."

"Mom . . ." He plucked nervously at the sheet covering him. "You said it wasn't 'that kind of divorce.' Well, what kind of a divorce was it, then?"

Stephanie took a breath, and came back into the room to perch on the corner of his bed. "We've talked about it before, Jeff. Two people just can't always get along. We married way too young and were from completely different types of families."

"But you're still mad at Dad?"

"Mad?" The question startled her. "No, of course not. Both of us were to blame for what happened. I was as much at fault as your father...."

"Do you *like* Dad?"

"Well...yes. I like your father just fine."

"Do you still love him?"

Her lips parted to say the simple, obvious answer, but it wasn't a simple, obvious question. Did she still love Alex?

She'd left him, deserted him, because she was seventeen, seven months pregnant and desperately frightened.

She'd met him in Boston during the years when her father had been a professor at Boston University. Will Randolph had taken an instant dislike to Alex, which had only fueled the romance of the forbidden. Alex had been everything forbidden, from his black leather jacket to the macho swagger. He was a grease monkey who didn't give a damn about books and intellectuals. Stephanie had lived the sheltered life of a professor's daughter, with landed money on her father's side to ensure she had the best of everything. She'd taken one look at Alex and tossed it all. Alex was life. And laughter. And noise, and sex, and danger, and fun, and Boston Coolers on hot summer afternoons.

Her head suddenly pounded with memories. Stephanie was staring at her son, but saw only a seventeen-year-old Alex. He was in a kitchen; it was night; she was sitting at a table, and he was leaning over her. His face was drawn and haggard, his eyes blazing with desperation. *You belong with me. Come back home with me, Boston. You love me. Tell me you don't. If you tell me just one time that you don't, I'll leave you alone....*

I don't love you, Alex.

Only she did. She desperately loved him, even when she said the words, even when she watched him walk away.

Love just wasn't enough, not when the real world started intruding. They didn't have a cent, and Alex was so defensive about anything to do with money. Her expensive wedding gifts, her inherited crystal and hand-painted china—Alex had resented all of it. He fiercely insisted that she take nothing from her father, but if it hadn't been for Will Randolph they would barely have had food for the table.

It wasn't just money that had torn her apart. Alex's family was a boisterous, close-knit clan. She was always the outsider. Alex was finishing high school at night and working long hours finishing his mechanics apprenticeship and they had little time together. Stephanie had no one to turn to but her father, and Will Randolph was always there to remind her of what she was giving up, not only college for herself but a real future for her child.

She'd loved Alex, but she was confused and alone and there was the baby coming. Alex expected her to wait. He expected her to believe in him, that he would provide her with a better life in time. But the baby was coming very soon, and her father kept insisting they move back home for a short period. He would get a nurse; she could go to college; the baby would have the best of everything. It wasn't the poverty for herself that brought her down, but the thought of privation for her baby. And maybe she'd really known that when she moved back home Alex would never go with her. Alex hated her father from the time Will Randolph had tried to have the marriage annulled.

Don't listen to him, Boston. Don't even listen to me. Listen to you, dammit. You can't hide every damn emotion forever. Do you even know what honesty is?

She knew. She'd gone deep inside her heart and knew. Alex didn't love her. He was a hot-blooded man, no virgin could have been more willing, and they'd both gotten caught.

For her it had been love. For him, sex. Hormones. Teenage boys were full of them. She'd gone home to her father, and Alex had come after her, night after night after night. He'd stopped once she told him she didn't love him. It should have been easier to say than it was, especially after her father had seen him going up to their old apartment over the garage with a redhead.

Stephanie had, that once, been totally honest with her emotions. Since then, the vulnerable feelings were better left tucked up in the corners of her mind and her heart. She knew Alex had never forgiven her for leaving him, for not believing in him. She'd crushed his pride, and he'd believed money mattered more to her than love.

But *her* pride had been crushed, too. If the circumstances were the same again, she'd act exactly as before. Yes, Alex had wanted her physically, but he'd also had a lot of pride about landing a "Boston Brahmin." He'd craved the image of a classy lady.

At seven months pregnant, she hadn't felt much like a lady. She'd been cumbersome and ugly and totally undesirable. She was frightened of giving birth and having her baby go hungry and felt despairingly sure that Alex didn't love her. The redhead had been the last straw.

"Mom?"

Stephanie blinked, and then immediately smiled reassuringly for her son.

"You didn't answer me. Do you still love Dad?"

She stood up from the bed, and bent over to tuck the covers around Jeff's chin. Fourteen or not, sometimes-man or not, her urchin could occasionally look angelic when he was tired. "I had a kitten once," she said softly. "I only had her a few months before she was killed by a car, and I adored that kitten, Jeff. If you asked me if I loved her now, I would say yes and I would mean it.... But it wouldn't mean much, because she's gone. We can't go back. There's no way to go back when you've really lost something. Can you understand that?''

"Sure."

Jeff yawned. Stephanie had the fleeting impression that he didn't understand at all. At least for the moment it no longer mattered to him. She tiptoed out of the room with the tray and carried it down to the kitchen. When the few dishes were taken care of, she slipped on a jacket and went out the back door.

The fresh air whipped at her cheeks. A dazzling autumn sun glinted down at her. Russet and amber leaves were starting to fall on the lawn. With Jeff laid up she'd have to do the raking this season.

She hated raking.

Stephanie closed her eyes, letting the brisk air surge into her lungs then out again. She was exhausted, but even feeling tired suddenly felt good. The life she'd made for herself and Jeff was good. She'd hurt, and worked hard and stumbled like everyone else stumbled from day to day, but she was making it.

Cobwebs cleared from her mind like magic. The night before she'd desired Alex. Probably she'd always wanted Alex, and maybe she was doomed to always want him. Still, she was no longer a naive seventeen-year-old virgin, disastrously willing to tumble in the front seat of a car.

And Alex might still want her, but a quick rush of hormones in the night would never erase the wound to his pride she'd given him. As he'd seen it, she'd left him for money. His "Boston Brahmin" had proved shallow.

The tough grease monkey she'd fallen in love with had been just that: tough and insensitive.

The allure of the forbidden . . . that allure could be very powerful. And very dangerous.

She knew better than to be tempted again.

Four

___

Let's see now. Boardwalk, Boardwalk ... With one hotel, you owe me $2,000."

"Mom." Jeff's cast was propped up on pillows. He made a special effort to look wan. "You haven't forgotten that I'm your only son and I have a broken leg?"

"At the moment I'm remembering all the times you failed to clean up your room. Two grand, hotshot."

Jeff shot his father a grimace. "I don't suppose you're in a position to float me a loan?"

Alex shook his head. Slouched in a chair, he had his stockinged feet comfortably propped on Jeff's dresser.

"She cleaned me out last time I landed on Park Place."

"Heck." Jeff sighed. "Okay, Mom, I guess I'm going to offer you all four railroads in trade."

"Which cost a total of $800 to buy. A long way from two thousand, kiddo."

"But it's a steady income every time people land on them," Jeff said persuasively.

"Chicken feed." But Stephanie accepted the deal. Even though her son was a chintzy bargainer, she loved him. Furthermore, he was clearly enjoying himself, which was enough to make Stephanie enjoy herself, with or without Alex in the room.

Actually, Alex was proving rather comfortable to be around. His laughter was natural, his grins lazy since he'd returned after dinner. Jeff's leg had swollen over the course of the day—to be expected, according to the doctor—but his crotchety mood had disappeared under his father's prompt takeover.

It was nine o'clock, and the sun had set two hours before. Since then, a card table had been set up next to Jeff's bed for the Monopoly board. Alex had the chair and Stephanie had brought up an ottoman to perch on. Unfortunately, she rolled the dice and got snake eyes, and winced.

"North Carolina Avenue," Alex drawled. "That's $1,275."

She leveled a scowl at him. "You realize you just collected from me the last time I rolled."

"I realize." It was just that point in the game when everyone had property and no one had cash. Alex's eyes shimmered with dry humor, waiting to hear the deal Stephanie was sure to come up with.

He'd returned from Boston to find the lady of the house exhausted from trying to anticipate Jeff's every need. Alex proposed the game to get them both off their feet, not because he had any expectations of enjoying himself. He was, though, thoroughly enjoying himself, primarily—and unexpectedly—because of his ex-wife.

She was sitting ramrod straight on the ottoman as if she was ready to serve tea to a duchess, but a strand of hair had come loose from its coil and had wantonly curled around her cheek. The paisley scarf that appropriately complemented her rust wool slacks was slightly askew, and she fancied herself a hell of a bargainer.

If he were in any way susceptible... But on the ride to and from Boston, he'd reminded himself of the exact reasons why he wasn't. Stephanie was a very dangerous lady when she let down her guard and started to play at being real. She was a lady capable of claiming love, without an ounce of trust to back it up. She was a lady who'd once taken his emotions, ripped them to shreds and laid them out to dry.

Still, the old animosity and bitterness were gone. He'd known it when she'd chortled while buying Boardwalk early in the game. There was a subtle irony in her pouncing on the most expensive property on the board. In real life, she even lived on Park. It fit her. Years ago, whatever made him think she could survive in an efficiency apartment, simply because of a small thing like love, was beyond him.

Maybe there was an ounce of that old resentment somewhere. Regardless, love wasn't on his mind at the moment, but watching his ex-wife look Sherman-tank determined to hold on to what she owned, was. Another strand of hair had sneaked out from the coil and lay like a whisper on her forehead.

Stephanie delicately cleared her throat, aware that Jeff was watching and expected her to be as playful with Alex as she was with him. "I'm about to make you an offer you can't refuse."

"I'm listening."

"First, these incredibly lucrative railroads I just stole from Jeff." She peeked up through her lashes. Alex was grinning. "And a free ride on Boardwalk any time you want it."

"Free ride?"

Jeff piped in, "Means you can land on Boardwalk one time without paying rent."

"You've landed on it every time," Stephanie reminded Alex persuasively.

Just like he'd fallen every time for that small stubborn chin and those alluring blue eyes. Alex had to steel himself. "I'd rather have cash."

"I would also sell you a Get out of Jail Free card, for a discount, plus two hundred dollars."

"I'm still listening."

"And I will go downstairs and bring you up a beer. That's my last and final offer."

Jeff chuckled. "Watch it, Dad. When money's short, you'll be surprised what she's willing to bargain with—taking out the garbage, cleaning rooms, a dinner at McDonald's..."

Kisses? Alex thought absently, and erased the errant thought from his mind. Damn it, why couldn't he be totally immune to her? She was her father's puppet. He hadn't forgotten that. The problem was his reaction to those little curling strands of hair, the off-kilter scarf and the faint violet smudges under her eyes.

When she was tired she'd always looked so damned vulnerable. He'd believed for so long that she needed a lot of holding, a lot of love, a lot of protection from the rough spots in life. As a kid he knew he didn't have money to offer her, but he'd had the arrogance to think he had something that mattered more. He thought she'd needed someone to teach her to feel, to coax her to express her feelings.

Foolishness. The lady was sheer brick, and anyone who had the nerve to propose the business deal she'd just made had enough guts to get through anything.

"Well?" she prodded. "What do you say?"

"I think your offer," Alex said slowly, "isn't worth a half pound of bologna. Now, if you were willing to go down and make me a Boston Cooler..."

He hadn't said it to be cruel, but he caught a flash of something in her eyes. Boston Coolers. The drink was made from ginger ale and ice cream, and they certainly hadn't invented it, but a long time ago they'd thought they had. Her eyes were suddenly the color of the highest sky, and the sweetest intimacy of a good memory soared between them.

Stephanie parted her lips to answer him, but for all of a second and a half there was total silence in the room. Then Jeff piped in, "Mom loves Boston Coolers, too, Dad."

"Does she?" He could surely hold the look as long as she could.

"Listen," Jeff said. "If you guys don't mind, I'll concede. You can still both go downstairs and have that Boston Cooler."

Stephanie's eyes flew to her son. "You're tired, honey?"

She could see he was. In minutes she had the board put away and the room straightened while Alex trailed Jeff to the bathroom, just in case he still had trouble walking around with the crutches. The boys were talking when she gathered up the glasses that seemed to have reproduced like rabbits in Jeff's room all day. Though she couldn't hear their exact words, conversation abruptly ceased when Jeff limped to the bed. She flicked a questioning brow to Alex, but he only motioned down the stairs, as if he would talk to her there.

"Night, sport."

"Night, Dad."

Stephanie hesitated one last moment in the doorway. "Honey, if you're the least uncomfortable in the night, just call...."

"I'll be fine, Mom. You just go down with Dad."

Jeff, she thought, if this is another of your subtle hints that you want me alone with your father... But it wasn't like that. Alex was waiting for her in the kitchen, one hand jammed in a pocket and the other raking through his hair. She waited for him to say something while she rinsed the few dishes and put them in the dishwasher. Finally she turned with the dish towel in her hands and shot him a humorous smile. "It can't be that bad."

"There's a couple of things I need to talk to you about."

Such gravity. "I gathered that." She turned back. "Do you want that Boston Cooler?"

"No. You want to sit on the back porch a minute?"

"Fine." She grabbed a jacket and slipped out the back door when he held it open. Moonlight shimmered down, clear and silver and shiny, on the dew-wet grass. She eased down on the top step and watched the white tail of a rabbit disappear helter-skelter into the neighbor's yard. Alex dropped down beside her, his elbows on his knees as he stared straight ahead.

"You're going to take this wrong," he began.

That would be nothing new, but for some reason Stephanie relaxed. Perhaps it was just seeing Alex unnerved for a rare moment. Alex was never unnerved.

Alex was an eye-to-eye person, blunt to the point of brusque, honest to the point of pain, but never a fumbler. He was fumbling. "Steph, about two years ago we seemed to have come to a similar conclusion, that it was time to talk to Jeff about the facts of life. You got to him first, I gather—at least he had a darn good idea of what's what before a gang of fool kids had spread their usual rumors."

One subject she hadn't been expecting him to bring up was sex, but as far as discussing it with Jeff, she'd had no hesitations. She'd never believed that just fathers should talk with sons and just mothers with daughters.

"Unfortunately..." Alex cleared his throat. "You must have decided you missed discussing something with him at that time, and maybe brought it up recently?"

"Pardon?"

"Boston." Alex stared at the sky. "You scared him half out of his wits. He's got this feeling he missed something major out of the whole deal."

She waited for him to look at her, but he clearly wasn't going to. "What on earth are you talking about?" she asked mildly.

"Don't get oversensitive about it. For heaven's sake, you didn't grow up around a bunch of brothers. There isn't a reason on earth why you would be familiar. More power to you that you even took the subject on, and you said it all right, that it was okay and natural and like that. This isn't a criticism."

"That's very nice. It would be even nicer if I knew what we were talking about," Stephanie said politely.

"Nocturnal emissions."

"Oh."

Alex's voice grated because he felt irritable—not at her but at his own awkwardness. Men were supposed to be able to handle these subjects a lot better than women. "Steph, the only people who call them that are women. They're called wet dreams, and if you'd said that, he would have known what you were talking about. I explained it to him a long time ago."

He stole a glance at her, but her hand had fluttered over her mouth. He couldn't see her expression.

"Boston?"

She stood up, her slim back to him. She seemed to be shaking.

"Boston?"

She started to speak, but laughter stole up on her. Alex was looking so alarmed. "Diapers..." She made her tone sound deliberately dismal. "Diapers and first grade and timetables were fine, Alex. Even sex was fine. Boy parts and girl parts and values and feelings and hormones—I can deal with that. Only in this past year, everything got so complicated." She threw up her hands in mock disgust. "Alex, I am just not prepared to mother a male adolescent. I keep mucking these things up—"

He cocked his chin on his palm, watching her. "I think you do pretty damn well," he murmured, feeling laughter bubble in his throat at her look of utter feminine frustration.

"Oh, no, I don't. Nocturnal dreams, or whatever they are, are just one thing. Heck, they just don't come up in private girls'-school education. But the worst, Alex, the worst—" The more glum her tone, the more he was laughing. Alex's laugh had always been catching, even worse when he was trying not to. She made her tone even more sorrowful. "—is jockstraps. I don't know what they're for. Well, obviously protection, but then there's this athletic cup business, too." She shook her head, starting to laugh with him. "Alex, I tried. I swear I tried, but I haven't the least idea in what sport a man wears what. Lord, is a boy supposed to wear something for tennis as well as for Frisbee? If you would please discuss it with him..."

Alex already had. At the moment, he was disarmed at the look of his proper ex-wife discussing jockstraps in a normal voice within hearing distance of her neighbor's yard. His Boston wasn't just laughing...she was laughing at herself, something she'd never been able to do before.

And by moonlight, her skin was clear and translucent and infinitely touchable. Her makeup had worn off. Being blond, she was naturally pale. He'd forgotten how sensitive she was about always wearing makeup to hide that.

He suddenly remembered very clearly how smooth and soft other parts of her body were. They were as white, as vulnerable and as elusive as moonlight.

His mood changed abruptly, but he managed to chuckle with her as she settled back on the top step beside him, her head leaning back against the post. "I never thought I'd abdicate any part of parenting, but darn it, Alex, you have my full permission to handle all those subjects from now on," she promised him.

"Hey."

"Hey nothing."

"You do a terrific job with him, and you know it."

"I used to. Or at least I used to feel I was a pretty good mother. But now—"

"No buts. No qualifications. What is this, Boston? You're a damned good mother. You can't seriously doubt that."

Heavens. A compliment? Her laughter didn't die so much as fade, like mist hovering back in the trees in early morning. Alex might be neither friend nor enemy, but there were certain things she'd never been able to share with anyone but him. Doubts faded in front of his assurance, and as far as the personal subjects affecting the raising of an adolescent—who else could she talk to but him? Alex was an earthy, physical man who had no prudishness in him.

Alex cocked a foot on the top step and rested his arm on his knee. "We need to move from jockstraps to dogs," he mentioned.

"Is that logical?"

"It seems to be to our son."

"Dogs," Stephanie echoed.

"He's got this idea, for one thing, that you need one. You don't travel a far distance, but you do travel in your job as auctioneer, and sometimes you get home when it's dark. Jeff is of an age where he's occasionally out for a movie at night and you're left alone."

Alex's face was all white and shadowy, strong bones and hollows in the semidarkness. He hadn't grown old, she thought vaguely, he'd just grown up. Moonlight played on the fan lines around his eyes, the furrow between his brows. He'd thought it so important to be tough when he was younger. Now, she realized vaguely, he was. Tough, as in impervious, because she hadn't the least idea what he was thinking. "I don't need any protection like a dog," she said.

"He thinks you do. In fact, he thinks you need an Airedale." Alex sighed. "Now look, Steph, I know you don't want a dog. For one thing, Jeff's gone all day and so are you. For another thing you've got a martinet of a housekeeper, and for another you've got white carpeting in that living room—"

"I'm thirsty," she mentioned and jumped up. When her jacket was hung in the closet, she moved into the kitchen, and without thinking started scooping ice cream into glasses of ginger ale. Boston Coolers.

"You'd have vet bills," Alex continued from his stance in the doorway. "You've got expensive figurines all over. Especially an Airedale—they're not small. One swish of the tail and you'd have a shambles. I told Jeff you wouldn't want a dog—"

"There isn't a reason on earth why we couldn't have a dog," Stephanie said smoothly, and handed him his Boston Cooler.

Dark eyes surveyed her over the glass as he took a sip. Alex had just listed a half dozen good reasons why she wouldn't want a dog. "You don't even like them," he said idly.

"All my entire life, I've wanted a dog," she said. "I like cats just fine. I had cats as a girl. But I always wanted a dog."

"Look. I was coerced into bringing up this subject, but there's no reason on earth why you should feel pressured. I don't even agree with Jeff. All I promised him was that I would talk to you."

"You did. And I'll get a dog for him. Tomorrow if possible."

The only light on in the kitchen was the one over the sink. Alex was standing in shadows, leaning against the doorjamb, and she could feel him staring at her. She should never have encouraged his laughter outside, because now she could feel a quiver of something pass through her. It was an aloneness between a man and a woman that she'd never felt with anyone except Alex, and certainly didn't want to feel with him now. "Alex, a dog is hardly a major thing," she said lightly.

He said nothing. She could feel his eyes on her like the bore of a drill, and she suddenly felt off balance. It was out of character for her to have wanted to make him laugh, out of character to know her makeup was gone and not care. It was also out of character for her to want a dog...and for a long time, she'd played a very careful character for her ex-husband.

She suddenly felt angry. The emotion came from nowhere. She motioned to the glass in his hand. "That's Waterford crystal you're drinking your Boston Cooler from. Did you know that?"

"No."

"I serve it to you whenever you have a drink in this house. You know why, Alex?" When he didn't answer, she responded for him. "I'll tell you why. It's because you always looked at that crystal like it was mud. It always irritated you. I brought the crystal and the sterling and the china with me to the apartment when we were first married. You hated all of it, Alex."

He still didn't answer, just stared at her.

"Damn you," she said softly. "Such an inverse snob. You thought I was the snob, Alex. It never once occurred to you that the china and the crystal were all that I had of the mother I never knew. I never explained it. I'll be damned if I have to explain that to anyone—not now, not ever. It was just..my mother's. And you're right if you thought I valued it. You were always so sure I valued things for themselves; you thought you knew everything about me. Damn it, I never even knew her. Things were all I had—"

His glass clunked on the kitchen table. Her voice was so soft she never dreamed it would incite a riot. She heard the ominous thud of his footsteps even as she was blinking back idiotic tears. She was over-tired. She hadn't slept a wink the night before. If she hadn't been so exhausted, she would never have brought it up.

But it was still no excuse for Alex to start riots. His arms slid under hers, and his mouth sealed hers silent, and she felt an agony of emotion in Alex that kept her still. He was angry. She could sense it. And Alex could be dangerous when angry.

"Damn you," he hissed. "Why didn't you ever tell me about your mother? And why the hell didn't you tell me you wanted a dog? You think I wouldn't have gotten you a thousand dogs?"

His lips fused on hers, and his hands clutched at her shoulders as if he wanted to shake her... except that he didn't. His fingers turned persuasive, molding her shoulders under his palms and then skimming to her back, her nape and into her hair. She could taste the sweet Boston Cooler on his tongue, and also something else—something warm and sweet and hot.

His kiss coaxed and demanded, enveloping her in pale mists and weakness. His thumb rubbed that special hollow in her collarbone; his lips trailed away from hers to tease her earlobe. Her wool sweater suddenly irritated her too-warm skin, and then his hands were there, slipping beneath it, soothing overheated flesh with fingers that knew just where to touch.

He had always known where to touch her, and when he shifted, drawing her to him, her whole body grew pliant. Her whole body fit perfectly to his. It always had.

"Alex..." She was trembling all over. She turned her head to avoid another kiss, but instead of breaking away she buried her face in his shoulder and wrapped her arms around him, holding on. The granite warmth of his chest was familiar and comforting. Her breasts felt oversensitive, tight and somehow protected, crushed against him. She was not going to fall into a chasm; she was not catapulting down mountains headfirst. Not as long as he held her.

Alex's hand slipped out from under her sweater; he smoothed the wool back in place, holding her, letting his lips rest against her sweet-smelling hair.

Her face finally lifted, and her eyes were framed by extraordinarily thick lashes, and her skin looked pale. "What on earth is happening to us?" she whispered.

"I don't know." At the moment he didn't particularly care. He'd destroyed her hair. He loved the look of her hair when he'd personally disheveled it. Half the pins were gone and soft strands tumbled around her temples. He pushed them back, soothing her. His heart was beating faster than hers, and he felt raw, as if half of him had been ripped away.

"We know better," she whispered unhappily.

"Yes."

"In all this time, we never before..."

"Yes."

"Alex, it's not like you still care anything about me...." She took a breath and stepped back.

His hand, in midair from smoothing her hair, dropped to his side. His dark eyes were suddenly as bleak as night as he studied her. An instinct told him it was critical she believed that he didn't still care. "We'll just have to be more careful it doesn't happen again," he said quietly, watching her.

"It's not as if both of us don't know better," she repeated, her arms crossed over her chest. She was rubbing her shoulders as if she were cold.

He turned, reached for his jacket and moved toward the door. "Boston," he said gently, "there isn't anyone here but the two of us. No one else is ever going to know that we shared a few kisses and it wasn't going further than that. Don't worry about it more than it needs to be."

She pounced on an excuse. "And we've both been overwrought about Jeff these past few days."

He didn't mention that Jeff was the last thing on their minds each time they touched. Digging his hand into his pocket, he tugged out his car keys. It was time to go, but he didn't want to leave her alone all distressed. "Airedales," he said suddenly.

That won the quick smile he'd needed to see. She relaxed, shaking her head ruefully. "I forgot all about the dog."

"You think about that overnight, and if you still decide you want one in the morning, I'll pick you up and we'll go dog shopping."

She watched out the window until his car lights winked off in the night. The kitchen clock suddenly ticked overloud, the only sound in the still house. She pressed her forehead against the cool pane of the glass, closing her eyes for a minute. After a time, her lips formed into a smile.

All right it was all darned foolish, but as Alex said, it wasn't going any farther. Heaven knew, they'd agreed on very little over the years. It struck her as humorous that at least they agreed on that.

"Dad, thanks so much for coming over this morning." When Will Randolph stepped into the kitchen, Stephanie affectionately threw her arms around her father. Tall and thin, he was dressed like the professor of economics he was—in an ancient tweed jacket and flannel slacks. She stepped back to study him. He was nearing sixty, and she always worried that he didn't get enough rest. The wrinkles around his eyes expressed the late hours he'd spent with books and papers, but this morning his cheeks were as red as an apple. The brisk walk had done him good.

"Just glad I didn't have any classes to interfere with your needing to go out. How's our boy this morning?"

"Jeff's doing fine. The only problem is keeping him down. For a few days that leg of his will swell if he doesn't stay flat, but telling that to him is like talking to the deaf. He won't stay still. I'll get you a cup of coffee...."

"I'll get it, I'll get it. Where is it you're going out this morning, anyway?"

While he poured himself a cup of coffee, Stephanie reached into the closet for her kidskin jacket. "To get a dog." She zipped up the jacket and tied a scarf around her neck. "Truthfully, Jeff would probably be fine alone for a couple hours, but I just don't feel right leaving him this soon after the accident, and it's a long drive to the animal shelter. Jeff just thinks he's Parnelli Jones on those crutches, and as long as you didn't mind coming over—"

"A dog."

Will said it as if he'd been forced to say a dirty word in mixed company. Stephanie had heard that tone of voice a lot over the years. Will had never spanked or scolded her as a child. He simply made her feel guilty with that certain tone of voice. It said she'd disappointed him. As a child she believed it was a crime worse than murder, and even now she still felt that way. She was his only family, his only link between years of loneliness, and she'd always known that. She also loved him as fiercely as he loved her.

This morning, though, his disapproving tone didn't affect her. Nothing bothered her. She'd woken up bubbling and happy for no particular reason and was simply enjoying the mood. Her smile was cheerful as she echoed firmly, "Yes. A dog."

"Don't you think Jeff is a little old to be in the 'animal stage'?"

"Yes."

"You realize what kind of work an animal is, and that it'll all fall on you. What with working and Jeff, you've already got your hands full—"

"I certainly do," she agreed.

"At least a cat is a much cleaner animal—"

"They certainly are."

Shivering from the frosty morning, Alex rapped once on the kitchen door and twisted the knob open. His eyes lit first on Stephanie. She looked terrific in a tan kidskin jacket and brown wool slacks. Her hair— for once loose on her shoulders—looked like a wave of palest honey. Except for a touch of lipstick, she'd forgone makeup this morning, and her skin was pure natural softness.

He forgot the cold, at least until his gaze traveled over to the sink, where Will Randolph was standing. Her old man hadn't changed. The pompous old goat still had cold blue eyes and a way of looking down on someone like he had cooties if his ancestors hadn't sailed on the Mayflower. Alex's background, of course, was considerably shakier than that. They shared an icy look and a frigid nod.

"I suppose you're responsible for my daughter's notion out of a clear blue sky that she wants a dog."

"Actually—" Alex's eyes traveled back to Stephanie "—I spent some solid time trying to talk her out of the idea."

Stephanie whisked the strap of her purse to her shoulder and hurried for the door. It was the first time those two had agreed on anything as long as they'd

known each other, but she wasn't going to be able to
breathe until they were safely separated.

"We should be back in a couple hours, most, Dad."

Her father's soft blue eyes pinned hers for a few
short seconds. So you're going off alone with him?
But remember how badly he hurt you. Remember that
redhead.

She hadn't forgotten the redhead. She hadn't forgotten a lot of things. At the moment she was simply
more concerned with Airedales, and her bright mood
had nothing at all to do with a few stolen hours with
Alex.

Five

Stephanie assumed Alex would drive until she stepped outside and saw the gleaming antique Pierce Arrow at the curb. "Wait until Jeff sees that one," she murmured. "I take it I'm driving?"

"Dog hair will never touch that car," he affirmed.

She chuckled, and took out her car keys. Over the years, when Alex had picked up Jeff, her driveway had held the Farinas, the Stutzes, the Cords. Jeff had brought her a newspaper article one time, claiming that Alex was the only man this side of the Atlantic who could make a '34 Dusenberg purr.

He'd come a long way from the leather-jacketed kid who'd bought a surplus World War II jeep for fifty dollars just to take apart the engine. People sought him out from California to Germany, and his name was on half the tickets Jeff collected for antique car shows. "Surely you're going to keep this one?" she asked him idly, glancing back at the Pierce Arrow. "She's such a beauty."

"That baby was badly neglected when I found her, but no, I won't keep her once I find her a good home."

"Has the baby been behaving?" she asked gravely, trying not to chuckle when he referred to the car as if it were an orphan.

"She has a slight carburetion problem."

"Ah. Other behavioral problems? No persistent coughs when you take her out? Taking her fuel and vitamins all right?"

"Boston?"

"Hmm?"

"You're in a very sassy mood this morning."

True, she thought whimsically. The night had left her high. She couldn't shake this mood and didn't want to. Perhaps it was from letting go of a little emotional baggage the night before. Perhaps it was sharing something rare and sweet with Alex that she never thought could happen again. Regardless, she wanted to be just where she was, next to him. Only for the morning, of course.

Her Le Baron zipped in and around the country roads. Frost sparkled in the early sun, reflecting the golds and russets of turning leaves. Alex slouched comfortably on the seat next to her, and occasionally prayed aloud when she took corners at full speed, making her chuckle. The wretched man always did have a good—if dry—sense of humor. "We'll get there in one piece," she assured him.

"I was just wondering how we were going to fit the dog with a seat belt—because he'll need one."

He turned his face to look at her halfway through the ride. She was blissfully high-spirited this morning and trying very hard to appear subdued, like a child afraid of being scolded for expressing her feelings. An odd feeling rippled through him that he only vaguely recognized as jealousy. She was a full-blooded woman who had every right to her moments of whimsical exhilaration. Some man, some time, was going to teach her that. He'd always believed it would be him.

Stephanie parked directly in front of the animal shelter. There was only one other car there. She stepped out and stuck her hands in her pockets, breathing in the crisp fall air.

A wrinkled old man ran the place, which amounted to his office, a stockroom and four long rooms where the dogs were separated by size and age. The old man promised them they could wander wherever they liked, then he leaned on his cane and started rambling to Stephanie, obviously lonesome for a chat.

While Stephanie politely lingered for the old man's garrulous prattle, Alex ventured into the first room on the right. A cacophony of high-pitched barks greeted him, so deafening that he chuckled. Puppies. He stuck in his finger in row after row of cages to have it licked to death by beagles, boxers, shepherds and heaven knew what kind of mutts—but by the time he reached the end of the line, he hadn't found a single pup with Airedale blood.

He was headed back out when Stephanie burst in. She was all but quivering with excitement, her blue eyes brilliant with laughter. "Alex, I've found him. The most beautiful Airedale—hurry! Two rooms over—"

It was difficult to hear her, since their arrival seemed to have roused every dog in the place. "Which cage?" he asked as she motioned him into the third room over.

"You won't need me to tell you—you'll know the minute you see him," Stephanie assured him. "Just go in. Alex—he's perfect!"

She waited in the doorway while he walked the rows. This room was obviously for larger dogs, and most were better than a year old. He passed a decent-looking collie, a hairy mutt cowering in the back of the cage, a growling Doberman, a mixed breed with a huge wagging tail, a sheep dog, another friendly-looking mixed breed...

"Alex, you can't be serious. Can't you tell an Airedale when you see one?"

He knew an Airedale when he saw one. "Perhaps you'd better show me," he suggested.

"Here," she said impatiently, and crouched down by the second cage. "The tag says his name is Walter. I know he isn't a pure-blood, but the man told me he was more than half. Just look at him!"

Alex did. She'd picked the hairy-looking mutt cowering in the back of his cage. If the dog's great great great grandparents had an ounce of Airedale blood, he'd be surprised. The dog was shivering violently, his tail curled under him, and he was moaning while every other dog in the place was barking up a healthy storm. Alex bounced down to his haunches beside Stephanie and cleared his throat. "Now, Steph, it's possible the old man might have imagined a little Airedale blood, if he thought that was what you wanted. I mean, his job is to find homes for these animals—"

"Alex, he *said*. And dogs are his business, he should know."

"Yes." Alex hadn't felt so helpless in a long time.

"He's perfect."

"Ah . . . yes." He cleared his throat again. "Maybe he'll look a little different to you if we get him out of the cage and you see him walk around."

"Great idea." She sprang to her feet and went in search of the old man. Alex was not surprised that the old codger didn't meet his eyes when he trailed in behind Stephanie to open the cage. When the door was opened, the mutt didn't want to come out.

"Look at him," Stephanie whispered. "He's all hunched over because he's been in that cage so long. Poor thing. . . ."

The poor thing was dragged into the owner's office, where he promptly sneaked under a chair facing a corner and hid there. Alex shot the old man a virulent glance, but he was busy talking only to Stephanie. "Now, I know he's a little on the shy side, but you wouldn't want an aggressive dog around families. He ain't got a mean bone in him, Walter don't. I promise you he won't bite nobody ever."

"He just needs love," Stephanie agreed. "And brushing." She whirled on the old man. "Don't you ever brush him? And let him out for a walk?"

"Sure I do, sure I do...."

"How many decades has he been here?" Alex cut in politely.

The old man cackled. "Your husband there sure has a good sense of humor."

Stephanie didn't bother correcting Alex's identity. "It's perfectly obvious the dog hasn't been here long or he would have been adopted before this. How much is he?"

"Normally, I have to charge twenty dollars, to pay for a pup's food and upkeep and cleaning the cages and so forth. But for you," he said warmly, "five dollars."

"You're kidding! Alex, did you hear that?"

"A steal," Alex murmured, and meant it. Yet again, he had to clear his throat, this time because he'd never imagined seeing his ex-wife's patrician fanny wiggling in the air while she ducked under the chair to get to a dog. To give the mutt credit he had good taste in women. He was slavishly washing Stephanie's hand. More difficult to believe, she was crooning sweet nothings to him.

Rather abruptly, she backed out, and when she glanced up at Alex's face her smile fell. "You don't like him, do you?"

"Honey..."

"Look. Just look. Just get down close to him, and then see. I mean, I realize he looks a little unkempt, but we'll brush him, Alex. And when you see his face close up, the whiskers, the big brown eyes..."

Against his better judgment, Alex crouched down and clicked his fingers for the dog to come. The dog looked dumbfounded. Alex sighed and moved closer. He checked out the soulful brown eyes, the hangdog whiskers, the matted coat, the cramped haunches, the general quivering mass of fur. Stephanie was staring at him, waiting. He could feel her waiting, like a kid waiting for Santa Claus on Christmas eve.

"Put out your hand," she urged.

He put out his hand. It was promptly washed from beneath the chair by a long, wet tongue.

"See?" Stephanie hissed.

"Boston, he's a great dog." Alex lowered his eyes and tried to put more enthusiasm in his voice. "Really a great dog. But he's hardly a pup, now. It's not that I don't think he's a terrific dog, but we still have lots of time to look at other dogs this morning. This one's going to shed constantly; I'm not real positive he's overbright...."

Her thigh touched his when she perched down next to him. "Dogs aren't supposed to be intellectuals, you know. Dogs are just supposed to be loving, and look at him, Alex.''

He was tired of looking at the dog, because looking at the dog reminded him that he had to face his son at home, the son who wanted an Airedale. He looked at Stephanie instead. Her mask was gone, her guard down. She didn't know or care that her thigh was pressed against his, that her eyes had a luminous, loving glow, that she very badly looked as if she needed to be made love to.

It was really an odd time to discover that he'd never been out of love with his ex-wife.

He stood up and reached for the wallet in his back pocket. Handing the old man a five-dollar bill, he glared at him.

The old man cowardly accepted the money and sidled over to the other side of Stephanie.

Stephanie took a hesitant move forward and then rushed the last two steps, throwing her arms exuberantly around Alex. The contact was short, and the flush on her cheeks revealed how rarely she felt free simply to express her emotions, but her chin was tilted up when she came back down from her tiptoes. She didn't regret it. ''Alex, Jeff'll love him!'' She turned away instantly. ''Walter, come on, darling.''

Walter didn't want to come. Walter was snoring under the chair. Swearing silently, Alex lifted the chair—the old man moved out of range very quickly— and jammed it down, and then picked up the fifty-pound dog. Stephanie held the door while he carried

Take 4 Books
–an Umbrella & Mystery Gift–
FREE

**And preview exciting new Silhouette Desire novels
every month—as soon as they're published!**

Silhouette Desire®

Yes... Get 4 Silhouette Desire novels (a $9.00 value), a Folding Umbrella & Mystery Gift FREE!

Elaine Camp's HOOK, LINE AND SINKER. Roxie Bendix was a reporter for *Sportspeople*. Sonny Austin was the country's top fisherman and the subject of Roxie's next interview. It wasn't long after they'd met that Roxie knew she would pay any price to make sure Sonny would not become the one that got away.

Diana Palmer's LOVE BY PROXY. When Amelia Glenn walked into Worth Carson's board room wearing only a trenchcoat and a belly dancer's outfit, she was determined to do her act. Worth had her fired, but Amelia didn't know that the handsome tycoon was determined to bid for her on his own terms!

Joan Hohl's A MUCH NEEDED HOLIDAY. For Kate Warren, Christmas was a time of emptiness—until she met handsome Trace Sinclair. And what had been a contest of wills began to change into something else, something only their hungry hearts dared admit . . . and would not let rest.

Laurel Evans' MOONLIGHT SERENADE. Emma enjoyed life in the slow lane, running a radio station in a small town. So, when TV producer Simon Eliot invited her to give a speech in New York she refused. So, why did Simon keep returning on weekends? And why did Emma wait so desperately for his arrivals?

SLIP AWAY FOR AWHILE... Let Silhouette Desire draw you into a world of real-life drama and romance as it is experienced by successful women in charge of their lives and careers, women who face the challenges of today's world to make their dreams come true.

EVERY BOOK AN ORIGINAL... Every Silhouette Desire novel is a full-length story, never before in print, written for those who want a more sensual, more provocative reading experience. Start with these 4 Silhouette Desire novels—a $9.00 value—FREE with the attached coupon. Along with your Folding Umbrella and Mystery Gift, they are a present from us to you, with no obligation to buy anything now or ever.

NO OBLIGATION... Each month we'll send you 6 brand-new Silhouette Desire novels. Your books will be sent to you as soon as they are published, without obligation. If not enchanted, simply return them within 15 days and owe nothing. Or keep them and pay just $11.70 (a $13.50 value). And there's never any additional charge for shipping and handling.

SPECIAL EXTRAS FOR HOME SUBSCRIBERS ONLY... When you take advantage of this offer and become a home subscriber, we'll also send you the Silhouette Books Newsletter FREE with each book shipment. Every informative issue features news about upcoming titles, interviews with your favorite authors, even their favorite recipes.

So send in the postage-paid card today, and take your fantasies further than they've ever been. The trip will do you good!

CLIP AND MAIL THIS POSTPAID CARD TODAY!

NO POSTAGE
NECESSARY
IF MAILED
IN THE
UNITED STATES

BUSINESS REPLY MAIL
FIRST CLASS PERMIT NO. 194 CLIFTON, N.J.

Postage will be paid by addressee

Silhouette Books
120 Brighton Road
P.O. Box 5084
Clifton, NJ 07015-9956

Take your fantasies further than they've ever been. Get 4 Silhouette Desire novels (a $9.00 value) plus a Folding Umbrella & Mystery Gift FREE!

Then preview future novels for 15 days— FREE and without obligation. Details inside.

Your happy endings begin right here.

Silhouette Desire®

Silhouette Books, 120 Brighton Rd., P.O. Box 5084, Clifton, NJ 07015-9956

☐ YES! Please send me my four SILHOUETTE DESIRE novels FREE, along with my FREE Folding Umbrella and Mystery Gift, as explained in this insert. I understand that I am under no obligation to purchase any books.

NAME _____
(please print)

ADDRESS _____

CITY _____ STATE _____ ZIP _____

Terms and prices subject to change.
Your enrollment is subject to acceptance by Silhouette Books.

SILHOUETTE DESIRE is a registered trademark.

CTD076

the mutt to the car. The mutt did not like cars. It took both of them pushing his hind end to get him into the back seat, after which he promptly jumped between the two front seats and started licking Stephanie's cheek as she turned the key in the ignition.

She chortled. "And he's going to make a great watchdog, isn't he?"

Alex slouched low in the passenger seat and considered what he could do to make this up to his son.

"Alex?"

"A terrific watchdog," he agreed.

Stephanie became subdued rather gradually. "Alex. I didn't mean to embarrass you in there."

"You didn't," he said shortly. She'd done far more harm to him than that. He'd caught glimpses of the woman he'd first fallen in love with. This was the woman who needed to love, who caught fire when her emotions were free, who was capable of giving without reserve or hesitation. He wanted that woman. He'd always wanted that part of her, wanted to watch that part grow and thrive and burst into flower.

She'd made a grave error in showing him that side of her again.

Her father took one look at the dog and said a faint, "Oh, my God," which was enough to upset Walter. He made a puddle on the floor. It had to be cleaned up. Then the dog required a bath, and that seemed to involve getting the whole house wet. Over lunch, Jeff politely brought a book to the table, with photographs of dogs so Stephanie could see what a real Airedale looked like. Jeff's friends came to visit in the afternoon after school. They all had disbelieving comments to make about Walter.

By the time Alex brought in Chinese food for dinner, Stephanie was fed up with sarcasm concerning her morning's impulsive purchase. And she was ready to take on any and all comers who so much as looked at her sideways. Alex was the one she really wanted to argue with, but Alex didn't so much as say a word to her. He just kept looking at her, with that hint of a smile, all amused and gentle.

After dinner, he and Jeff settled in front of a football game with a bowl of popcorn. Stephanie slipped on a jacket and went outside with a rake to vent her frustrations on the leaves. The dog followed her as far as the back porch, and after a thorough petting, flopped down with a contented sigh.

In spring and summer she appreciated the massive old elm and maple trees in the backyard. In the fall she had a sea of leaves ankle-deep. Today's piles were adequately deep so that she could vent a lot of physical frustration. The dry leaves crackled under her rake. The last rays of the sun turned them to shiny gold and copper and rust.

She briskly made one neat pile, then stopped to take off her jacket. Even though night was falling and the air was crisp, raking was hot work. She made a second pile and then a third. Her neighbor from across the fence paused to chat with her a minute. She could hear kids shouting as they rode their bikes down the road. As the sun set, people locked their houses up tight and sent their kids to bed. Stephanie's eyes had become accustomed to the darkness and she was unaware how late it was until she heard the back door open. The porch light flicked on, and Alex stepped out from the shadows.

"You're going to work all night?" he asked mildly.

"I might." Her voice was crisp.

He sat on the top step, his hand reaching out idly to stroke the dog. She continued to rake, her pile growing bigger and bigger, but it wasn't the same with Alex sitting there. He had one hand on the dog and the other cocked under his chin, watching her. The sky was a rough black velvet, just like his eyes.

"Jeff asleep?" she asked finally.

"Yes."

"I do have another rake, you know," she mentioned politely.

He shook his head. "You're the one who needs to vent the frustration, Boston. Not me."

"And what's that supposed to mean?"

He said nothing for a minute and leaned back on his elbows stretching out his legs. She had a scarf on her head and wore an old sweater. She wasn't looking her best, but she was certainly thoroughly covered. It was Alex who made her think she was revealing parts of her body to him as she lifted, bent and raked. Uneasy thoughts dangled through her consciousness. Vaguely she felt that she was about to be singed by fire, when there was none anywhere around, just the darkness and the crackle of leaves.

"Do you like the dog?" he said gently.

The damn dog. Her blood pressure rose promptly. "Yes, I like the dog, but if anyone else says one more blessed word—"

"Then what do you care, Boston? What do you care what anyone else thinks?"

She propped the rake against the tree and whirled on him, hands on hips. "It's not that I care what anyone thinks. It's that Jeff wanted an Airedale. You let me get that dog when you knew darn well it wasn't even remotely related. You could have at least told me! Now I've disappointed him—"

"Honey." Alex stood up lazily and walked down the steps. "I love our son just as much as you do, but forget Jeff for a minute. Jeff has a whole lifetime to raise Airedales if he wants to."

"He still..." She dropped her hands. "Darn it, I just feel foolish," she said testily and turned away, grabbing the rake again. "I'm not in a habit of feeling foolish, of making silly, impulsive decisions, of..."

"You like the dog?"

"I already told you. I *love* the dog. Love has nothing to do with anything. I shouldn't have..." The rake was whisked from her hand and propped against the tree, faster than she could blink. Alex whisked an arm under her thighs. The world abruptly tilted and a bold male scent became part of the night. Suddenly she was pitched into a high pile of leaves.

"What do you think you're—" she sputtered. "You're insane. You're..."

An armful of leaves drifted over her head, and when she brushed them from her eyes to see, Alex had another armful.

"Don't you dare!" She flipped over and tried to scramble away, but not before the leaves hit her. In self-defense, she gathered a handful and prepared to pitch them back. "Alex!"

Her voice was a shout, not a whisper. "Throw them, Boston. Be silly. Be foolish for once. What do you care?"

"Of course I'm not going to throw them. I—"

Leaves drenched her, coating her hair with crackle. Mindlessly, she retaliated with the handfuls she had and heard Alex's hearty laugh. "More!"

"More? You're nuts. You've wrecked this whole night's work. I'll have to do it all again—" Another shower of leaves, at least half of which made their way down her back. This time she bent over and picked up two armfuls, pelting the whole lot at him. Then she threw a second bunch at him. And a third and fourth, and suddenly it was all mixed up in laughter and she was only trying to be mad. She was warm all over, giddy warm, bracing warm.

She was still laughing when Alex tackled her, and they both went down in a breathless tangle of shadow-tipped gold and russet. His weight was a shock for a few seconds, but she had another surprise when she brushed the leaves from her eyes and opened them on

Alex's face. 'He was braced on his elbows, his legs locked over hers, and the smile was gone from his lips. His lashes looked sooty, and they barely shielded the very clear, stark wanting in his eyes. Danger pulsed through her bloodstream. She tried to spring up, but the movement only brought her thighs tightly against his arousal, and her breasts now chafed against his chest. She hadn't budged him. One couldn't move granite. "The leaves," she said breathlessly. "They're itching."

"I know," he murmured. "Sorry, Boston, I just don't care." His lips dipped to her nose, then her cheek, then her temples. Slow, lazy kisses. There was no need for speed when the lady was well pinned.

"Alex . . ."

"My foolish lady needs kisses, rewards for being impulsive, and an apology that's a thousand years overdue. It's a little one, for not being man enough to understand you a long time ago." He added softly, but firmly, "It won't go too far, Boston. But don't try to stop me for a minute or two."

Her mouth suddenly felt dry. His hovered over hers and then descended, his tongue dipping inside her parted lips, soothing away the dryness. His hunger was real, and it beckoned her own. She wound her arms around his neck. The whole world smelled like man and autumn and earth. She could see the crystals of stars, yet her eyes were closed.

It all happened so fast. His leg shifted between hers, and his thigh rubbed deliberately against her softness. A match exploded in the darkness. His hand slid down her body possessively, kneading her breast until the soft flesh hurt and ached and chafed from the layers of clothing between them. Another match. His lips burrowed beneath her sweater, his teeth nipping at that tenderest of skin by her collarbone.

Maybe the fire had been building for days, maybe years. It wasn't a simple thing. It had never been a simple thing for Stephanie to want any man so much that she neither knew nor cared about time or place. She felt angry and very foolish, but the exhilaration kept coming, abetted by the suddenly harsh sound of Alex's breathing. "Honey, if you have the least intention of calling this off..."

His whole body tightened when she ran her hands down his back, first to his taut buttocks, then to the backs of his thighs. In that instant when Alex was off balance, she pushed against him and he collapsed into the bed of rustling leaves. Her lips trailed after him, finding his. One last time, she thought. Somehow, it felt inevitable, and that in itself was delicious. His mouth was delicious. Her fingers climbed his jeaned leg and rubbed until she heard Alex's responsive groan, and that was delicious, too.

"Boston."

"Shut up, Alex." If she'd wanted another warning, she was certainly capable of giving one to herself. Instead she traced his smooth white teeth with her tongue. She lifted up and straddled his hips and let her breasts sway and brush against his chest. Stephanie knew exactly what she'd invited and Alex suddenly surged up, lifting her up with him. Then they were standing in the darkness and the leaves fell from their clothes and hair. His mouth leveled hard and rough on hers. She was kissing him back, just as hard.

"We're going inside." His voice was gravelly. No one could have eyes that black. They were fierce and his face was carved in rigid, harsh lines. If he'd been a stranger Stephanie would have been terrified of him. Only he wasn't a stranger, and she knew exactly what he looked like when his control was gone.

"Yes," she murmured in agreement.

"Not upstairs. Jeff could hear and wake up—"

"I know... and the living room is too open. Alex, there's no place!"

But he found one, behind the lock of a door, darkness, steps... a blanket somewhere. She assimilated very little beyond cool, dark privacy, a faint hint of light coming from a distance, and total stillness after all the rustling leaves and night sounds. Some part of her brain registered that somewhere behind the closed door the dog was moaning, unhappy at being deserted.

It didn't matter. Nothing mattered. Her sweater was being swept over her head, her bra unsnapped and slid down her arms. For a moment Alex used the straps to hold her arms captive while he spread lush, lingering kisses on her throat, her shoulders, the first swell of her breasts. A sound welled up from her throat, weak and yielding, invading the total quiet that surrounded them.

He looked at her when he took off his shirt. Black diamond eyes held hers until desire soared through her, and then his hands gently slid down her bare sides to the snap of her pants. A vague uncertainty suddenly distracted her. It was the way he was gazing at her, as if savoring the memory for the long winter nights and lonely summer days ahead. Only she certainly wasn't as beautiful as his eyes told her she was. She wasn't . . . treasure.

"Alex . . ." Her hands covered his before he could bare the last of her. "I'm not like I was," she whispered. "I'm not so slim anymore; there are stretch marks."

"You'll have to show me." His palms glided down her bare hips and thighs, chasing the pants until they were pooled on the floor. He lifted her then, and she felt the graze of a wool blanket, heard the creak of old springs as he urged her down. He touched his lips first to hers, then trailed lower over throat and breast, down to her navel, down to stretch marks. "These are what you're worried about?" he murmured gravely.

He kissed the silver thread lines—there were two—then kissed around them, then held her still while his lips traveled in widening circles where there were no stretch marks at all, just tufts of blond softness. She whispered a hoarse cry; he paid no attention.

In time, his body slid back up, covering her newly trembling flesh. His gaze took in the glowing blue sheen of passion in her eyes without smiling. "Were you worried about anything else?" he murmured.

She buried her face in his throat for answer.

"You're more beautiful than you were, love...." His kisses suddenly escalated, showering on her face and throat. "And you were more beautiful then than a man could handle." His tongue whipped across the tip of her breast until the flesh ached, swollen and full for him. "And I have never, ever stopped wanting you."

He stood up to tug off the last of his clothes. It was only a moment before he was back, a moment to savor the intimacy of his warm hair-roughened body against her softer flesh. He parted her thighs, wrapped her legs around him and thrust with aching slowness into her hot, damp core. His mouth muffled the gasp in her throat, a kiss that treasured her sound of pleasure. Her body seemed to have turned into foam.

Alex, the boy, had been a passionate giving lover. Alex, the man, knew more and was no longer content with the simple, fierce, sweet satisfaction of need. He wanted diamonds. He demanded rainbows. He coaxed her skin to silk; he wooed her senses to the fine edges of madness. And when she was clinging to him, murmuring his name mindlessly, he showed her sky.

Afterward he held her, shifting her on top of him so her head lay on his chest. He wrapped his arms around her first, then covered her with a blanket, and they both lay there, breathless, sleepy, exhilarated, quiet.

"I'm too heavy for you," she murmured.

"No. Never. Although—"

She heard the faintest sleepy humor in his voice, enough to make her tilt her head to look at him.

"—I think it just registered where we are." His eyes flickered to the room around them, the shelves, the couch, somebody's forgotten lamp. "I didn't just make love to you in a basement," he assured her.

"More comfortable than the MG used to be," she said gravely.

"I don't even remember taking you down the stairs."

He was so clearly bothered by it, she laid her finger on his lips. "It didn't matter then and it didn't matter now," she said softly.

He tilted his head to press a kiss on her temple. "I like to think of you surrounded by soft sheets and down pillows and satin covers and..."

"And I like believing you wanted me so much that you didn't know or care where we were," she whispered back.

"You know you were that wanted," he said hoarsely.

"So were you."

He then smiled. "You have leaves in your hair."

She laid her cheek against the soothing throb of his heartbeat again. "So do you."

"I like your hair styled with leaves."

"Thank you."

"I like you naked. In fact, I love you naked."

A flush warmed her cheeks, and she shifted so she could easily look at him. Only suddenly she couldn't. Her lashes splayed on her cheeks like champagne dust. "Alex, I want to tell you something."

"Tell me." His fingers spread, combing through her hair.

She wanted to lean her cheek into his palm, take comfort from the warmth and strength of his hand, stay here with him like this forever. Only it couldn't be like that. She had no illusions that making love with him changed anything in the long term. She'd made love with him because she wanted to, because she'd needed to. Because she was foolish. Because she wanted him to forgive her for a long time ago. Because there were too many years stretching out ahead of her like a barren desert.

All those becauses, and there was still one she didn't dare face. She felt shattered, frightened. That "one more time" had affirmed what she'd needed to know and didn't want to know: there was no other man who stirred her like Alex. No one who ever had, no one who ever could. She had no gift to give him of equal value but honesty.

His smile died while watching the changing emotions on her face. He lifted her chin with his cupped finger. "Tell me," he said softly.

"I just...wanted you to know something." She touched his rough cheek. "Alex, I don't blame you for her, for...the redheaded girl. A long time ago you accused me of being immature and spoiled, and you were absolutely right. I'm as much to blame as you— if not more so—for everything wrong that happened between us." She hurried on in a rush. "And that's all water over the dam again, nothing I'm trying to bring up again. I've just wanted to tell you that for a long time. That I understood, and never blamed you for the... girl."

His palm, in the process of smoothing back her hair, stilled. The look in his eyes would have singed everything in its path with a fire burn, and he said nothing for a moment. When he did, his tone had the disarming murmur of silk. "The... girl," he echoed. "I always knew your father had told you something when he convinced you to move back in with him. I just never knew what it was."

"She doesn't matter," Stephanie repeated, and meant it, but she found herself curiously waiting, studying Alex's face.

"You want me to deny that she existed?" he said quietly.

She shook her head. "No." Her heart whispered, yes, oh, yes.

"I won't do that. Deny she existed. Ever, Boston."

"I didn't ask you to!" For some idiotic reason, she felt the prick of tears in her eyes. "I was just trying to tell you that I was to blame, not you. I'd hurt you and badly; we'd both hurt each other—"

"And that was all a century ago. Put your smile back on, little one." He flipped the blanket off her, and cool air rushed over her bare skin. His palm slapped her bottom, a playful pat that almost stung. "Shower for you? Somehow I don't think you'll enjoy sleeping with leaves in your hair, nor have an easy time explaining them to Jeff in the morning."

A woman who didn't know him better might think nothing was wrong. He teased her while he dressed, chased her up the stairs, kissed her before he left. But everything was suddenly wrong, and he didn't really kiss. His mouth was cool and hard and angry.

She felt brusquely, achingly deserted when he was gone, and stood in the kitchen for a long time, her arms wrapped around her clothes, the dog leaning against her side. She'd wounded him, she knew that. That had never been her intention; she wasn't even sure how it had gone wrong so fast.

Obviously it had been a terrible mistake to bring up the redhead. She'd never done it to hurt him. In her heart, she'd known they had to settle the issue of the other woman before they could go on. And from her heart, she'd wanted to erase the last hint of old guilt and blame between them.

Because you love him, said a bleak voice in her head. You've done it again, Boston.

Six

I'm sorry I had to call you in, Stephanie," George said from behind his massive teak desk. "I know you'd planned on spending this entire week with your boy."

"It's all right," Stephanie murmured absently. Seven days after the accident, Jeff was all but doing cartwheels with his crutches and wasn't about to miss her for a few hours, even if Alex hadn't been there this morning.... Alex. She focused determinedly on the photographs in front of her.

"If I'd been more familiar with the Louis XVI period... But we've never landed an estate quite like this."

"Hmm."

"One of the difficulties is going to be what an un-usual kind of home it is. It's overpriced even for the high value of estates around Echo Lake. That won't make it easy to push."

"Hmm." George had the irritating habit of talking whenever she was trying her hardest to concentrate. The picture in front of her showed a renovated Louis XVI house, secluded on several hilly acres near one of White Mountain's ski resorts. Photos of the inside of the house revealed twenty-two-karat gold ceiling moldings, twelve-foot ceilings, antique marble fire-places, silk wall coverings and German crystal chandeliers. The furniture that came with the estate was equally priceless.

She loved it. All of it. And work was exactly what she needed to keep her mind off other things.

"If you don't think you'll have time to handle it, I could put Val on it—"

"Don't you dare."

George smoothed back the invisible hair on his bald head, and smiled. If he'd complimented Stephanie by telling her she was the only one he'd even considered for the job, she would have been annoyed. Stephanie didn't handle compliments well; she just handled challenges well. And George, in his own fussy way, liked to tease her. "You were complaining two weeks ago that your work load was unmanageable."

"Oh, hush, George." Crossing her legs, she set down the folder of photographs and grabbed a legal pad. "Let's get down to specifics. Probate arrange-

ments, mortgage values, last insurance evaluation—
have you got a list of artwork? And do we have time
to sell the home as a whole, or are we dealing with an
auction arrangement for the contents?''

Two hours later, she climbed into her car to drive
home. Traffic had picked up on the Friday afternoon,
and she had a locked and well-stuffed briefcase on the
seat next to her—for which she was tempted to murder George. He'd insisted she could leave it over the
weekend when he knew darn well she couldn't stand
to leave work hanging. She could do it once Jeff was
asleep.

She hadn't missed her job in the past week because
she'd loved the time with her son, but that was never
to say her work wasn't important to her. After a few
hours in the office, she felt refreshed, challenged and
ready to face a few frustrations again. Jeff was climbing the walls at his enforced inactivity; the dog was
proving worse to raise than a fifty-pound baby; and
Alex, of course...

Alex shouldn't have been on her list of frustrations. He'd been enormous help this week. The fau-
cet in the bathroom no longer leaked. Her storm
windows were washed and in place. He could understand Jeff's geometry, which she certainly couldn't.
He'd brought in dinners so she wouldn't have to cook,
cohosted the barrage of teenagers who'd visited Jeff.
In fact, the only helpful thing he hadn't done in the
past week was touch her.

It would have been very helpful if he'd touched her.

Rationally, of course that was ridiculous. Any display of affection around Jeff would have given their son galloping hopes for a reconciliation, and Jeff already had his head filled with plenty of those. And as far as any dreams she'd been harboring about futures, she'd obviously blown them, the instant she'd mentioned the redhead.

Why, she didn't know. She did know she was hurting, and badly. Maybe she'd always hoped he'd deny that he'd been seeing the redhead. Hell, of course she'd wanted him to deny it. That he hadn't only confirmed what her head already knew. It had cost her a lot to bring it up, and she'd been willing to only because she knew she had to put pride behind her if they had a prayer of starting again. She'd risked that pride. And he'd trampled it exquisitely. Since they'd made love, he'd treated her like a priceless goblet of Waterford crystal.

Flicking a glance in the rearview mirror, she straightened the cowl neckline of her violet cashmere sweater-dress and practiced a distant smile. Alex hated that kind of smile. Behave yourself, Stephanie, she thought.

She forced herself to relax, which worked until she pulled into the driveway. The Pierce Arrow was gone from her driveway. This time he'd driven a Lagonda LG45, and she was irritated first because she knew the names of his damn cars these days. Her irritation was spurred when she spotted three legs sprawled on the cement; the attached bodies were hidden by the car itself. There were only three legs, because the fourth was in a once spotless white cast now covered with grease stains.

Stephanie vaulted from her car, shut the door with a crisp click and bolted for them. On cue, the two males rolled out from under the car on their body trolleys.

Alex was wearing a pair of worn jeans, a shirt-sleeved sweatshirt and a smudge of dirt on his cheek. The jeans and shirt had seen decades come and go. She felt his eyes whisk from her Italian leather pumps to the tasteful dress to her patrician nose. Abruptly, his eyes met hers and dropped.

For one swift instant she'd caught a sizzle in his eyes. For one swift instant, she'd seen the muscle tighten in his jaw, a flare of some brilliant harsh light pass between them. Then abruptly there was nothing. A cool remote dismissal that twisted like a scissor slice, and his tone might have been trying to soothe a schoolmarm. "Now, Stephanie..."

Stephanie gave him the same look she'd give a worm...or the look she'd give a man who'd made the mistake of using her. Damn it, it hurt to share something as precious as their night together and then be ignored. She was tempted to tap him on the head—hard—with a hammer. He couldn't ignore that, could he?

Instead, her heels tapped out a more civilized form of frustration on the pavement as her gaze darted to her son. Jeff's bruises had disappeared beneath a solid coating of grease. A once favorite red plaid shirt was now black with a tear in the sleeve. "Now, Mom," Jeff said uneasily. "I know I was supposed to stay in the house, but we were just fixing the suspension system. Don't start yelling at Dad. This was all my idea."

"You have never once heard me yell at your father," Stephanie reminded him crisply.

Her son exchanged glances with his father, and both rather abruptly lurched to their feet. "I'll finish up," Alex told Jeff. "You go get cleaned up and give me a minute with your mother."

"I don't want you guys arguing about me—"

"Jeff," Stephanie said gently, "no one's going to argue about anything. Really. I promise you." She waited until Jeff was behind the closed door of the house before whirling on Alex. "And I'm certainly not going to argue with you. I'm going to kill you."

"Ah." Alex propped open the long, shiny hood of the antique car and buried his head inside. If he didn't look at her, he would be fine. He promised himself he would be fine. All he wanted in life was some nice, kind, docile woman who didn't make love like a siren and then stab him in the gut.

She'd been looking for a fight for three days, and she wasn't going to get it out of him. She'd done enough "forgiving him" for that redhead. No one and nothing had hurt him like that since he'd run into Stephanie at seventeen. She didn't know him and never would, and his tone could have buttered toast. "Well, you're right, Boston. He was supposed to be resting that leg, not performing gymnastics beneath the engine of some car...."

"You've got that right."

"Besides that, he's been stalling about making up his schoolwork, which I probably should have been having him do...."

He was stealing her lines. She scowled at the flexing muscles of his back as he reached into the engine. Something went ping, and his hand groped behind him...inches from the oily wrench he was clearly reaching for. She gingerly picked it up and fed it to his hand like a nurse for a surgeon.

"Apart from which, you really don't want him anywhere near cars, and I don't blame you for that."

Her brows formed feathery arches. She was aching to argue with him—to do anything to show him she didn't care—but she hadn't expected it to be so easy. "What do you mean, I don't want him anywhere near cars? That has nothing to do with anything, Alex. It's just the timing; you *know* his leg still has a tendency to swell when he's on it too much."

"As far as that, he was lying flat, which meant there was no pressure on his leg." A plonk sounded; the wrench was aimed back at her. She took it and set the greasy thing back down. "I only took him out here to discourage him," Alex said flatly.

"Why? You know he loves cars."

"So do most fourteen-year-old boys. But he's been talking about being a mechanic, so I figured I'd take him out here and show him how tough and dirty a job that really is." Alex's head twisted to stare at her momentarily. "You don't have to worry that I'd ever steer him in that direction. My son isn't going to be any grease monkey all his life. He's going to Dartmouth. I've always wanted him to go to Dartmouth. He's going to make something of himself, a lot more than I ever did."

"That is possibly," Stephanie said frigidly, "the stupidest thing I've ever heard you say."

"And what's that supposed to mean?"

The sudden snap in Alex's eyes was exactly what she was looking for. It wasn't that she wanted to fight with him so much as she couldn't stand the indifference. All week long she only had to be near him to suffer hot flashes. "I meant just what I said. That was a stupid thing to say. If he wants to be a mechanic, he can be a mechanic. As far as his schoolwork goes, of course I care that he does well. I want him to do his best at whatever he takes on, but that's not because I have some ridiculous notion that he has to go to Dartmouth."

"Every man in your family has gone to Dartmouth for generations," Alex snapped, and buried his head in the engine again. "Hand me the three-sixteenths, would you?"

"So? And what the devil is a three-sixteenths?"

"A wrench. And don't give me any nonsense about it not mattering to you that Jeff follows the same tradition."

Bending down, she surveyed the litter of tools by Alex's toolbox. The wrenches did have numbers on them, and finally she chose the right one, feeling flustered. Damn tools. Engines were even worse. All the wires and metal-looking boxes and complex coils of an engine... She liked furniture. She liked twenty-two-karat ceiling moldings and Royal Doulton china. "I not only don't care if he follows the same tradition; I have no intention of pushing it," Stephanie said sweetly. "It would be fine by me if he were a mechanic."

"Well, it isn't by me. I want better for him. He's going to work at a job where he doesn't have to get his hands dirty."

"Hands wash. At least yours always did." She peered over his shoulder, not because she had any interest whatsoever in what he was doing, but just to see.

"Don't get any closer. You'll just get that dress dirty," Alex said irritably. But he already knew it was too late. Her perfume was wafting toward him like poisonous nectar. Damn it, even teenage boys didn't get aroused from just the smell of perfume. The woman had warped his sanity, when he knew he'd rather be standing there arguing with her than being anywhere near a nice, kind, docile female.

"Dresses wash, too."

"Not that one." Gruffly, he cleared his throat, his tone muffled. "That dress looks nice on you."

For a moment, the only sound in the driveway was a robin chirping from a nearby elm. As compliments went, it lacked a certain poetry. So it was ridiculous how the blood suddenly danced up and down her veins. "Thank you." She took a breath. "But about Jeff—"

"There's nothing else to say about Jeff. He'll be a grease monkey over my dead body."

"That's one option," she said politely.

"He can be a lawyer. Or a doctor. Or an engineer—"

"Or a mechanic. Or a ditch digger. Or an electrician."

"I don't even care if he teaches—"

"I don't care if he's a carpenter."

"Boston, will you shut up? He's not going to work with his hands."

"Listen, you addlepated snob—" The back door slammed, and when she saw a newly cleaned-up Jeff approaching them, she pasted a brilliant smile on her face. Only Jeff seemed less interested in her smile than the gritty wrench in her hand. He suddenly beamed at her.

"You're helping Dad? Gee, Mom, I always figured you'd like cars if you'd give them a chance, and there's no better teacher than Dad—"

"Lay off your mother. It's not a crime if she doesn't like to get her hands dirty," Alex snapped from beneath the hood of the car.

Stephanie glared at his muscled back. He had no idea how close he was to being throttled. "It was never that I didn't want to get my hands dirty—"

"You've been arguing," Jeff said worriedly. "And here I thought you guys were getting along so well. Heck, Mom, I always thought if you'd just try to understand Dad's work..."

Alex peered out of the engine to settle an ice-cold glance at his son. Jeff promptly clammed up, but Stephanie could see the look in his eyes. A headache suddenly hammered in her temples. Jeff actually believed she was to blame for never showing interest in Alex's work.

"Damn it. If I just had four hands... I can be out of here in ten minutes if you'll just hand me that, Jeff."

Jeff seemed immediately to know what Alex was talking about, but Stephanie reached out a hand to stop him from picking up the grimy part. It wasn't to help Alex but for Jeff's sake that she picked it up herself, and was rewarded when her son grinned at her as if she'd done something marvelous.

"Now stick it back in for me, would you, sport?" Alex ordered, his voice muffled.

She looked blank. Jeff, with a wink, motioned to where she was supposed to put the thing and she did so...except that it didn't exactly fit. In fact, it dropped into the engine with a clatter, and for some horrible reason, cold oil splattered everywhere.

Alex's head reared up like a lion in a cold rage, his face peppered with smooth black spots. The rage in his face died when he saw Stephanie's cashmere dress now polka-dotted. Jeff was looking at his mother as if he'd just identified the worst klutz this side of the moon.

"Boston..." Alex's voice had lost its acid crispness; his tone was low and hoarse, and the muscle working in his jaw was tense, his eyes liquid black. "I'm sorry. Really sorry. I'll buy you a new dress. Just like that one."

"Don't be silly, it doesn't matter," Stephanie said swiftly and reached down for a rag—but the rag was even more oily than the stuff on her hands. She smiled wanly at both. "Jeff, you can clearly handle this a thousand times better than I can."

She escaped into the house, letting the storm door batter closed behind her. The silence of the kitchen enfolded her like protection. She moved to the sink, near tears for no sensible reason whatsoever. She'd failed Jeff, that was all. She'd wanted him to see that the ruined relationship between his parents was never because she hadn't been willing to try her hardest.

She flicked on the faucets and reached for the soap, which was foolish. Plain soap didn't do a thing for greasy hands, and it certainly wasn't going to dent oil stains on her cashmere dress. Behind her she heard the steady thumping of a tail, and turned to find Walter in the doorway.

She bent down, and the dog loped forward to deliver a fat wet tongue on her cheek. "I *did* try," she whispered to the mutt. "I did. I made mistakes, Walter, but those were never because I didn't love him. I've changed—he could at least see that. I was so darn sure he'd changed too...but he hasn't. He hasn't, Walter. The only thing he ever wanted from me was sex, and like a fool..."

Like a fool she'd fallen in love with him again. She'd felt herself being dangerously lured into wanting the forbidden again, because they were grown up now, and not so foolish and not so young, and because she still wanted him. It still made sense when he touched her. She'd tried for so many years to date other men, but it had never worked.

The back door popped open, and Jeff's head peered in. "You okay?"

He'd clearly been instructed to make sure that she was. She straightened and smiled. "Of course I'm okay."

"I forgot to tell you, you had a call this morning. That Brice dude, something about symphony tickets this Saturday. Like tomorrow? He was afraid you might have forgotten."

She had, completely. Her spirits lifted promptly. It was exactly what she needed, not only to get away from Alex but to be around another man. Any other man.

The next afternoon at five o'clock, Alex pulled into Stephanie's driveway. Before he even had the car in park, Jeff was bounding out of the house, winging away on his crutches as if ghosts were chasing him. A wry twist of a smile stole the tension from Alex's face,

Jeff piled into the front seat, jamming his crutches in the back. He was wearing a suit coat, white shirt, tie, and jeans cut off at the knee for his cast. "Step on it, Dad," he said hurriedly, his eyes darting back frantically to the house.

Though he didn't know it, Jeff was going to suffer a very long evening. "We're in a hurry?" Alex said mildly. "I thought I was an hour ahead of schedule. The symphony doesn't start until eight, does it?"

"No, but traffic could be terrible and it's a long drive to Boston." Jeff turned to his father, and his eyes widened in alarm. "Dad, don't you know how to do a tie at your age?"

Alex's free hand went instinctively to the yellow and gray tie at his throat. His white shirt chafed at his throat; the gray suit jacket felt claustrophobic on his shoulders. Alex hated suits, starched collars and classical music, in about that order. There were very few reasons in life he was willing to suffer through any of them. As it happened, Jeff had called him in Boston at noon with a desperate plea to be taken to the symphony.

"Dad, how old is that suit?"

Alex hedged. "A reasonable age." There was a lot he was willing to do for people he loved. Shopping wasn't one of them.

"I guess your hair looks all right, anyway."

"Thanks, sport." Alex's tone was dry, but he shot his son a studied look. Jeff's cheeks had the flush of a ruddy peach; he couldn't seem to sit still. Guilt surrounded him like a halo.

"You look great," Jeff assured him. "I just particularly wanted you to look your best. You know . . ."

Alex cleared his throat. He had to give his son every chance to come clean. "Care to explain it to me again why we're using your mother's season tickets? Since you always go with her, I can't imagine why you asked me. You didn't make it very clear on the phone."

"But she couldn't use them, and I love Shostakovich, and they were just sitting there. I told you. And like, it's nice for just the two of us to do something together, right?"

"Of course it's all right." Except that they'd just spent the past two weeks doing things together. And to accommodate this whim of his son's, Alex had driven from Hanover to Boston the night before, now Boston to Hanover to pick him up, now Hanover to Boston for the symphony, and back yet again to Hanover tonight to deliver Jeff back home.

Alex hadn't hesitated. There really was a lot he was willing to do for the people he loved.

"Dad," Jeff said firmly, "I know you think you don't like this kind of music, but you probably haven't heard it in a while. Like I didn't like it when Mom first dragged me to these things, either, but now I think it's pretty good. It's just like rock or jazz or country, or any other kind of music. You have to let it in, you know?"

"It doesn't matter as long as you like it, sport," Alex said absently, and then deliberately paused. "Something's obviously bothering you. If you'd like to talk about it . . ."

"No, no. Nothing's bothering me. Nothing at all. Everything's going great." Alex looked sideways at his father. "Dad, you're going to at least try and like it, aren't you?"

Alex cleared his throat. "Sure." He'd like violins when hell froze over.

The closer they got to Boston, the more difficulty Jeff had sitting still. By the time they both climbed out of the car in the parking lot and Jeff grabbed his crutches, his face was the color of wax.

As expected, they were nearly an hour early for the performance. Their seats were in the eighth row, numbers three and four from the aisle. These days, people dressed pretty much as they pleased for the symphony, but it seemed to be one of those nights when a slow stream of elegantly dressed people gradually wandered down the aisles. The men were dressed in everything from dark suits to tuxes, the women in furs and silks with jewels blinking from their throats and wrists, perfume trailing after them.

A gathering of highbrows generally made Alex uncomfortable but not tonight. Tonight he found a comfortable fit for his shoulders in the chair, crossed one leg over the other and watched Jeff become increasingly agitated with a mixture of frustration, amusement and guilt. He would have liked to put his son out of his misery, and he didn't like the thought that Jeff had to learn some things the hard way. If the son had been any less like the father, Alex could have chosen a different tack.

By the time the Boston Philharmonic was warming up, Alex felt compassion overrule his better sense. The lesson had surely been learned. Jeff was chewing his lip and risking whiplash, because he kept twisting to see behind him.

"Couple of things I'd like to talk to you about," Alex said lazily.

"Now?"

"Now," Alex confirmed. "First, I think you'd better get rid of those girlie magazines you've got under your mattress before your mother finds them, don't you?"

Jeff turned a delicate shade of crimson.

"And second, there'll undoubtedly come a time in my life when you can outfox, outthink and outmaneuver me, Son. More power to you when that time comes. In the meantime, though, you can save yourself an awful lot of mental grief by remembering that I'm on your team. Talk, Jeff, don't hide a problem." Alex paused, clearing his throat. "There's only one problem on earth where I can imagine I wouldn't be on your side. I know this may be difficult for you to believe, but I'm really quite capable of handling my own love life."

Jeff was trying to listen, but couldn't. Alex's eyes were peeled to the top of the aisle. Abruptly, the crimson in his face blanched to white. "Dad, I've got to talk to you," he whispered urgently.

"Do you?"

"Only there isn't time. And I'm afraid . . . you're going to kill me." His eyes darted to his dad's. "Soon," he said glumly.

Alex followed the trail of his son's gaze. Several people were entering the theater. An old diamond-studded dowager, a young girl with a date, two women in velvet capes . . . Behind them, was a tall blond man with a neat beard and glasses, wearing a black suit. On his arm was a champagne blonde, wearing a butterscotch silk dress that flowed around her figure. Amber dangled from her ears and throat. She looked expensive, delectably touchable, and unbelievably classy. Alex's eyes fastened hard on her slim fingers coiled on the man's arm, before he turned to his son.

"No, I'm not going to kill you," Alex said mildly. "But your mother is. Which is why you're sitting on the other side of me, temporarily out of harm's way."

"The party sounds fun, but I don't think so, Brice," Stephanie murmured. "I'd rather not be late getting home tonight."

"You said your ex-husband had Jeff."

"Yes, but they're only going out for pizza and a movie; they won't be late and I don't know if Alex plans to drive all the way back to Boston yet tonight." She reached aisle eight, seats one and two, took a step toward the inside seat and glanced around with a ready smile for the people next to them. Dark eyes met blue. She froze.

"Stephanie?" Brice said behind her.

The seat was cushioned. She was grateful. Her purse slid out of her hand to be tucked neatly by her feet. By the time she leaned back up, her lips were set in the poised curve she reserved for federal disasters like earthquakes. Or hurricanes. Or ex-husbands showing up out of magicians' hats. And yes, she noticed her son cowering on the other side of Alex. She faced first her date. "Brice, you've met my son, haven't you?"

"Jeff? Of course, I ha—"

"Say hello, Jeff," Stephanie ordered quietly.

"Hello, Mr. Rivers." Her son was trying to rush on, his voice as small as a mouse's. "Mom, we kind of changed our minds about the pizza and movie—"

On a rare occasion, Stephanie ignored her son. She spoke only to Brice. "And sitting next to me is my ex-husband, Alex Carson. I don't believe you've met him—"

"I—no." She gave Brice all kinds of brownie points. The bones in his cheek went rigid; he darted her a look of irritation, but his arm was promptly extended. "Brice Rivers," he said to Alex. "This is unexpected, I must say."

Both hands met in front of her nose. The shake was swift, mandatory and over quickly. But not so quickly that she didn't notice the real difference in the men's hands. One was manicured, white, with long, thin fingers, a professor's hand—which was Brice's occupation. The other one was callused, sun-weathered and firm, and so absolutely definably Alex's.

"I apologize for the awkward situation here," Alex said quietly to the other man.

"No problem, no problem. We're all here to enjoy the music, aren't we?" Brice said heartily.

The lights dimmed, and the music started with a crash of cymbals and trumpets. Shostakovich, as Stephanie knew well, liked to start out with a bang. Her heart was thudding, and the drumming in her ears had nothing to do with the orchestra. She felt like the white of an Oreo, tucked between two men's stiff, dark shoulders.

After that first glance at Alex, she didn't look at him again. She'd seen enough. One look had shown her the starched collar digging into his neck, the grim lines around his mouth, the way his hair had been rake-combed by his hands, his horrible tie. Alex always chose terrible ties. Store-bought suits refused to accommodate his shoulders. And she knew exactly how Alex felt about classical music.

The shock at finding him here faded, and the hurt of the past few days dulled, replaced by a helpless burst of compassion. At the first lull in the music, she leaned over him and plucked Jeff's arm.

Her son didn't want to look at her.

"How could you do this to your father, Jeff?" she said furiously.

Trumpets clashed again, oboes bellowed, French horns glinted in the semidarkness. For twenty minutes there wasn't a sound but the powerful music of the Russian composer. To her left, Alex's hand suddenly muffled a yawn, followed by Jeff's exasperated, "Dad! Try!"

Seconds later, there erupted a murmur of Stephanie's laughter, followed by Alex's masculine chuckle.

Brice's shoulders tightened. Jeff took the first safe breath of air he'd had in hours.

Seven

———

Brice's headlights winked a good-night as Stephanie hurried to the front door. Though Brice had made good time driving from Boston, Alex and Jeff had arrived ahead of them.

As she unbuttoned her cape, she peered around the corner of the living room. Alex was there, leaning negligently against the mantel. He'd thrown off his jacket and unbuttoned his shirt; his tie was draped over a chair. His dark eyes fastened on hers, and an odd little chill ran up her spine. She rather rapidly ducked back toward the closet and reached for a hanger.

"All right. Where is he?" she demanded.

"Asleep."

"Where's the dog?"

"Up with Jeff."

"I'll get you a beer, Alex—"

"Thanks. No."

Well, she needed something. With regal grace, she crossed the room to the decanter of wine on the table by the couch. She poured a glass, set it down as if already forgotten and distractedly fussed with the cuffs of the dress instead. "I don't know what either of us was laughing about, because it wasn't funny, Alex," she said darkly.

"I agree."

"Our son..." Her voice connoted a dire future for their mutual progeny. Her heart was unfortunately thinking about that quick burst of shared laughter between them.

Laughter could do some very strange things to one's common sense when only shared by two. The rest of the evening had been an uncomfortable blur. Alex had been next to her, intimately next to her in the darkness. The brush of his arm, the smell of him, the sexual awareness of him had disturbed her. During the intermission, Brice had trailed her to the lobby to get a drink and done the usual things dates do—bent closer to hear above the madding crowd, used a casual hand at the small of her back to steer her around people. She'd felt Alex's eyes following her like lasers and felt the guilt of an adulteress, when damn it, she'd done nothing. Actually, she'd never done anything with Brice; and Alex had hardly been celibate all these years. She had no reason at all to feel guilty.

She not only felt guilty, she felt wretched—and vulnerable. During the ride home with Brice, she'd snapped at him for suggesting her son was a little out of hand.

Their matchmaking son, of course, was drastically out of hand. And as long as she could keep her mind on Jeff, she could keep it off the man leaning against her mantel with the thick, dark hair and the oddly bitter smile.

"I can't imagine how Jeff conned you into attending that symphony. I know you hate that kind of music." She waited for the explanation, but he didn't say anything. "Alex, we have to do something about him."

"I have," Alex assured her. "I don't think he'll be in a hurry to meddle in other people's affairs again."

"Well, that's something. But I still don't understand what he expected to accomplish."

"I do." Through hooded eyes, Alex watched the elegant blonde pace in front of him in a swirl of butterscotch silk. He hadn't forgiven her... for a lot of things. None of that mattered once he'd guessed why Jeff had been trying to coax him to the symphony. It wasn't only jealousy that prompted Alex's actions, but compassion for his fellow man. Stephanie was a dangerous woman—dangerous, untrusting and troublesome. In all good conscience he couldn't let her loose to hurt someone else. In fact, if her date had dared to walk in with her, Alex would certainly have escorted him out again, maybe with a black eye to make sure he got the message across.

Damn it, he loved her.

And at the moment, he was relishing her nervousness. She picked up the glass of wine, again set it down, and slid her hands into the silky pockets of her dress. "Jeff seemed to feel," Alex said mildly, "that your date was a creep."

Color surged into her cheeks. "Brice is hardly... He's a very fine man!"

"Have your wine," Alex suggested.

"I don't want any wine!"

Ah. She was clearly in one of her more rational moods. "You're right, of course. He looked like a very nice, quiet professor. Like your father—proper and always right, the kind of man whose word you'd never doubt for a moment."

Funny, how little words could nick. Stephanie stopped pacing long enough to glare at Alex. "I've never doubted your word about anything," she said in a low voice.

"Haven't you?"

Stephanie caught the glimpse of black fire in his eyes. As if she'd mistakenly walked into the cage of an angry cougar, she suddenly felt trapped, in danger and vulnerable. She looked away. "We were talking about Jeff."

"Actually, I thought we were talking about trust. Stephanie?"

She turned.

"Jeff did have to learn a lesson about interfering in other people's lives. He did and that's done. Don't, though, waste any time blaming him for my being there. I went by my own choice, and I went knowing you'd be there with another man."

It was just a little bomb, but little bombs in small quiet living rooms could be just as dangerous as big ones. Stephanie felt the shrapnel from her temples to her toes. "Alex..." She licked suddenly dry lips, and then lifted her chin. "If you thought that I didn't have the right to see anyone else just because we slept together one time..."

"The issue," Alex said with deadly softness, "is what it meant to you. Not my feelings but yours."

"All week," she started heatedly. "All week you haven't once let on that you cared one iota. All week... If you'd just once said you cared—"

"Cared? Cared is a tepid word, honey. It doesn't remotely relate to what I feel for you. It never has and never will."

She could feel his anger vibrating across the room, as intimate as a touch, as private as a locked bedroom door. Conflicting emotions assaulted her. Fear that he'd unleash that anger on her, when she knew he wouldn't. Anxiety that she'd hurt him again, when she'd done nothing to hurt him. And love, the most powerful emotion. She desperately wanted to soothe him, to erase the exhausted wrinkles around his eyes, to change the harsh lines of his mouth to ones of softness. Only she couldn't do that and protect herself from a man capable of badly hurting her. "What do you want from me, Alex?"

For a moment there was silence. "Do you love me?" he asked finally.

In a thousand years, she couldn't have expected the question, not there and then. Her blue eyes mirrored the answer, but she couldn't say it.

"Ah, Boston," he said softly, "how I'd like to shake you, and if for a minute I thought it would do you any good, believe me I would."

"Alex—"

"So damned afraid to express your feelings. You think I don't understand? Emotional honesty hurts. Only we've got to start there, and I have to know what you're feeling, not guess at it." He straightened and glanced at the chime clock on the far wall. "It's late."

She let out a breath, grateful that he was dropping the subject. Confused and upset, she murmured, "Yes."

"And I'm not driving back to the city tonight. I'm too damned beat. And the Inn is full—homecoming weekend."

Her eyes met his for all of thirty seconds. Trust. He'd accused her of lack of it, when it had always been there. "All right," she said calmly. "You know where the spare room is."

She didn't turn on the light in her bedroom, just closed the door and slipped off her dress in the darkness. The light from a sliver moon shone in through her window. A keening wind was whipping newly bared branches against the panes. It was the kind of night to snuggle next to someone under a comforter, and feel warm and safe against the threat of coming winter.

She took the pins from her hair, halfheartedly brushed it, took off her slip and bra and burrowed under the covers. It was so late, and she was tired, but instead of sleeping she listened to the wind howl.

An hour later she heard the knob to her door turn. It was the smallest sound in the darkness, almost imperceptible, a sound she'd been trying to convince herself she hadn't been waiting for.

Her head turned to the shadowy form of the man at the threshold. He wasn't wearing any clothes. "Alex?" she murmured, but the surprise that should have been in her voice wasn't.

Without a word he closed the door behind him, then latched it. He crossed the room to the foot of her bed and stood looking down at her. Her hair was silvery in the darkness, her face softly blurred and her throat white and slender just above the sheet. Her eyes shone in the night like the shimmer of two luminous stars.

She looked as young and vulnerable as she had when she was seventeen, and that angered him. Unresolved feelings of desire, anger, frustration, mixed in his head. They'd both changed, grown up, matured. All the real trials that had once torn them apart were gone now, part of the past where they belonged.

Everything had changed, except for the most fundamental thing of all: trust, faith in him. She had the memory of a redheaded woman he had no idea she'd been harboring. He'd had the choice to defend himself, hadn't and wouldn't. Ever.

Alex had no intention of arguing the subject of redheaded women with her. He had every intention of teaching her something about emotional honesty. At the deepest core he had to believe she trusted him. He desperately needed to believe that.

And he had to prove it to her. If that meant using anger, he would. If that meant courting the area where she was most vulnerable, he would do that, too.

He reached down, and pulled slowly at the comforter from the base of her bed. It wouldn't give for a minute. She was holding it, and then she released her fingers. Inch by inch, he pulled down the covers to reveal her smooth white breasts, her satin belly, the shadowed curve of her hips clothed in a wisp of silk and her thighs.

She was suddenly trembling all over. "I'd like to believe," she murmured softly, "that if I told you 'no,' Alex, that you wouldn't force..."

His voice was velvet steel. "I'm going to make love to you."

She shook her head. "Yes. But you wouldn't. If I..."

Words suddenly wouldn't pass her thickened tongue, the dryness in the back of her throat, when he slid down beside her. It was dark, too dark. He was more shadow than clean lines, more stranger than lover. She was afraid.

The first contact of bare skin to bare skin was electric...the pain of sharp current, the pleasure of heat. Alex's mouth layered on hers in the darkness, a kiss of such pressure that her head was forced down into the pillow. Her heart felt like the fluttered beat of a trapped dove, her breasts, hands, skin unbearably vulnerable.

In time, he lifted his head, dark eyes boring into hers. His thumb traced the line of her cheekbone almost too gently. "You hurt with it for years, didn't you?" he whispered. "So good at hiding your feelings, honey, even from yourself. When you brought up that woman, I think you even believed you wanted it forgiven, forgotten. Only you fibbed, Boston, because you haven't forgotten it at all."

"No—"

"I'm going to make love to you," he murmured. "There isn't a damn thing you can do to stop me. Know that. We're going to start from there, because I sure as hell don't know where else to start. Let it go, honey. Get angry, let it out. Tell me how you hurt with it."

There was silence, and then from nowhere, an arm lashed at him. It missed, because he ducked, searing his mouth on hers, wrapping his arms and legs around her.

She was angry, suddenly terribly angry. She was suddenly frozen at seventeen, the night her father had told her about his...girl. She was seventeen, and spoiled and confused and inadequate and frightened, and no, maybe there wasn't a chance in hell they could have made it anyway but damn it she'd loved him. She'd loved him with every cell, every atom, every gene, from her toes to her crown, from her heart to her head. That he'd slept with someone else had split her in two.

Her fists hit his back. The blows didn't lessen the pressure of his mouth on hers. Terrible tears flooded her eyes, seeped beneath closed eyelashes when she tried to hit him again. She was angry, not hurt.

A whimper of pain tore from her when his mouth slid from hers to the most vulnerable part of her throat. He lingered there, at the pulse beat, then moved down to her breasts. She wanted to lash out again. She wanted to physically hurt him as she'd been emotionally hurt; she badly wanted to keep nothing in her mind but that redhead. But there were only two of them in the darkness, not three.

There'd never been more than two of them in bed, nothing else, no one else. The world didn't exist, and neither did place nor time. Just Alex. The more rough, the more desperately uncontrolled her response, the more his touch softened, turned tender, as if rewarding her release of anger. He was coaxing any choice of emotion she dared to express, and demanded her honesty.

Her spine arched when his tongue trailed the underside of each breast. His palms cupped both, covered both and his teeth so gently nipped their swollen tips. His lips drew and drew, draining her of hurt, energizing her with a fierce, desperate heat. Not heat. Need.

"Alex, I don't want . . ."

"The hell you don't." Then he whispered softly. "And you're going to want more, Boston. You're going to die with it before I'm done. You're going to shout what you really feel. . . ."

He wasn't . . . gentle. He wasn't kind. She'd looked for years for a gentler man than Alex, a kinder man. She'd found them.

The only problem with any of those men was that they weren't Alex. His tongue touched her where no other man had touched her. He wouldn't listen to her pleas. She felt alternately as soft as a kitten and as wanton as a whore. Alex demanded all of that and more, whispering to her, daring her to soar higher. He wanted her nails denting his skin. He wanted her softest kisses. He wanted her brazen touch on his body. He wanted her murmurs in the night.

Stephanie's body was as sleek as damp silk before his thigh slipped between hers, before he towered over her. When he thrust into her, she wrapped her legs around him and felt anger and love and fear and lust and passion and sweetness and tenderness. No one else had come close to making her feel anything as wild and powerful as Alex did.

She cried out; his mouth absorbed the sound. She knew she had to be quiet because of the son they'd conceived a long time ago. But she didn't want to be quiet. She wanted to shout and cry and the thrusts of his body brought her closer to ecstasy, but denied her the peak. "Tell me," he whispered.

"I want you!"

"Not that...."

"I love you, Alex, damn you, damn you..."

Her body shuddered in explosion. She heard Alex's exultant moan, his love pouring into her. She felt that love, felt the moisture of it, the realness of it.

The shadows of the room gradually took substance again. The wind was still keening. Alex was stroking her hair, placing fierce kisses on her cheek, her nose, her temple. "Don't," he murmured, "try and take it back, love. Not after that."

She shook her head, wrapping her arms around him. "I wouldn't."

When her body grew cool, he tugged the comforter up, nestling it around both of them.

"Jeff," she said suddenly.

He shushed her with kisses. "I'll be gone when he wakes up. I'm holding you now."

She needed to be held now. She didn't fight him.

A month later, there was a glistening sheet of the first snowfall on the ground. Will Randolph stood with his hands on his hips in Stephanie's living room. Perched on a ladder, his daughter was fixing streamers from curtain rod to curtain rod. Furniture was pushed against the wall, figurines put away. The dog, he noted without surprise, was snoring from his usual position at the corner of her white couch. Jeff's stereo was sitting on the carpet, and a dozen colorful album covers stared at his grandfather. "Those people aren't wearing many clothes," Will observed.

Stephanie chuckled. "Those covers are mild. You should see some of the albums he brings home."

"I can't think of a reason on earth why people can't make equally good music wearing clothes—if those creatures are actually people. And if that's actually music on the records."

Smiling, Stephanie climbed down from the ladder and surveyed the living room critically. "You think that's enough decoration?"

"For a circus," her father assured her.

With a rueful look, she walked over to press a kiss on his cheek. "Now, Dad. I promised Jeff a boy-girl party months ago. He's never asked me for anything like that before. I have to do it right."

"You don't think he's a little young for a mixed-sex party?"

"I think he's a lot too young." Stephanie grabbed the leftover rolls of crêpe streamers and headed for the kitchen. "But I'd rather know his friends and have them free to come here than have Jeff off someplace where I didn't know what he was doing."

"I just think kids grow up too fast these days," Will muttered as he trailed her into the kitchen. "His cast off yet?"

"Two days from now."

"I thought Jeff told me Alex was coming for this thing tonight."

"He'll be here." Stephanie clicked shut the refrigerator door, her gaze averted from her father's as she started fussing with a tray of relishes. "I've got to get dressed soon, Dad."

"Sit down with me, and stop working for five minutes."

"Only five," she compromised, and blew a wisp of hair from her cheek as she sat down across from him. She'd known the minute he brought up Alex that her father had more to say. It had been coming for weeks.

"Alex has been around a lot more than he used to be," Will started slowly.

"Since he moved back to Boston, it's easier for him to see Jeff."

"To see Jeff," Will echoed. "Funny, but the day I took Jeff to a movie, Alex's car was still in the yard."

But that occasion, she wanted to say, had been rare. Alex had left her the night of the symphony, and stayed away for an upsettingly lonely week. He'd come back one fine fall morning when Jeff was in school. He'd come back, and he'd looked at her. They'd been together in bed minutes later.

There'd been about a half dozen other times, just like that one, but it wasn't easy to arrange privacy around their son.

The strain of their clandestine relationship was beginning to show on Stephanie. She'd lost several pounds and the soft smudges under her eyes gave her skin a vulnerable translucence. When she and Alex came together it was like fire. Neither wanted to talk, but each time Alex left her she had the feeling he was waiting, waiting for something from her when she'd given him all she had. She'd spoken of love; he hadn't. For her, it wasn't just sex, but there didn't seem any way to bridge the silence between them.

"He isn't good for you, Stephanie," Will said bitterly. "He was never good for you. He used you. You were an innocent young girl, and he used you and hurt you—"

She shook her head. "I hurt him just as much," she said quietly.

"He's trying to start something again, isn't he? For a while, I thought you were pretty serious about this Brice fellow—"

She shook her head again. It was useless to explain that Brice was pale to Alex's color. "Dad? You remember the night a long time ago, when I agreed to move back in with you?"

"I'm not likely to forget it."

"Do you remember what you told me?"

Will's shrewd eyes lit on his daughter's. "I told you exactly what I saw," he said slowly. "I drove by the old place. There were steps leading up the side of the garage to your old apartment—"

"Yes."

"It was September and still warm. And bright outside. He had an arm around the girl. She had red hair. She was wearing shorts. She was young. And when they got to the top of the stairs, he put his arms around her. He kissed her. She was laughing."

"Yes." Stephanie's chair clattered back as she stood up. "I know. I don't even know why I asked you. Dad, I really do have to get dressed. Jeff's friends are going to be here in an hour."

But she paused for a long moment to fiercely study her father's face. She wanted to see a lie there. She wanted to believe that her father had made up the story to get her out of a marriage he'd always hated. It would have been a lie of love, and having a son of her own now, Stephanie could well understand how a parent could lie to protect a child.

But she saw no guilt on her father's face. She saw clear blue eyes and integrity and honesty. Finally she turned away.

Will stood up. "I'll get out of your way. Hope your party goes well."

"Thanks, Dad."

"Give my best to Jeff."

"I will."

"Sweetheart?" Will hesitated, staring directly at the window. "Maybe I should never have told you about that girl. You know, I never did it to hurt you."

"Oh, Dad, I know," she said softly.

Will didn't seem to hear her. "The thing was, when you were seventeen, there was no one but me to protect you. It was never that I hated Alex, but that I was so sure he wasn't right for you. That he'd hurt you."

He cleared his throat. "I know I interfered more than..." His voice trailed off.

In the fussy way he had, he picked up his coat, methodically buttoned it, arranged his scarf just so. "Maybe I made some bad mistakes as a father. Maybe I didn't," he said gruffly. "When I think back, I was just so desperate to know what your mother would have done. I never knew—but I do know that she'd look at you now and do something about your being unhappy. If it means anything..." He cleared his throat again. "I won't interfere again. Nor pass judgments. And I think you'd be surprised how fast I can accept any man who makes you happy."

Stephanie gave him a fierce hug and her best smile. She'd never expected that from her father. Accept Alex? Years ago, she'd have given him diamonds for that acceptance.

Now, it was too late. Alex wanted her, but he no longer seemed to love her.

She was hard-pressed to put herself back in a party mood, but she had to for Jeff. Actually, he made that reasonably easy to do, as he trailed after her while she was trying to finish dressing.

"You're not going to hang around too much, are you?" Jeff asked for the third time.

"I promise, I won't 'hang around' too much."

"And Dad. You'll tell Dad when he gets here..."

"I'll make absolutely sure he understands he isn't to hang around too much, either."

"It's okay if he shows some of the guys his car."

"I'll tell him that, too."

"Just no standing in the doorway when we're all dancing."

Stephanie couldn't resist turning around from her dressing-room table to tweak her son's nose. "Jeff," she said gravely, "we will do our absolute best not to embarrass you."

"Embarrass me? You guys don't embarrass me, I didn't mean that. Heck, all my friends like you. *I* happen to like you. I just..."

"I know, honey. You just want everything to be right."

Jeff stopped running a comb through his hair long enough to survey her outfit with a man's critical eye. She'd settled for simplicity: a coral silk blouse, white crêpe pants, a gold chain belt. At Jeff's coaching, her hair was down, and simply pulled back with combs. He claimed she looked too much like a chaperon with her hair up. "Julie'll like that color."

"Julie? Who is this Julie you keep mentioning?"

"Just one of the girls coming over." He said with a grin, "You know, you look nice, Mom."

"If that's shock I hear in your voice..." Stephanie started indignantly.

The doorbell rang below, and they both surged for the stairs. In spite of his crutches, Jeff reached the front door first. After listening to a steady hour of chatter from her son, Stephanie was bewildered to find him totally mute when he opened the door.

The girl on the porch didn't look so daunting. Wearing designer jeans and a mulberry-colored sweater, she had a sweet smile, naturally pink cheeks and dark, curly hair. "Hi, Jeff," she said shyly.

"Hi."

Then nothing. Stephanie cleared her throat and stepped forward, rather flabbergasted at her son's brusque manners. "Hi, I'm Mrs. Carson. Come on in. You're the first one here, and that's terrific. You can help pick out some music to get started."

"My dad's going to pick me up at eleven."

"Fine. And your name is...?" Since her son seemed to have turned into stone.

"Julie. Julie Baker."

Ah, Julie. Stephanie should have known. All children should be so easy to entertain. The two seemed content just to stand and stare at each other. Stephanie tactfully moved away. "I've got some things to get ready in the kitchen."

"Fine, Mom."

"Nice to meet you, Mrs. Carson."

She was still smiling to herself when the back door opened some twenty minutes later. Alex popped in and winced at the loud sounds coming from the living room. "Sorry I couldn't get here before this. Traffic was a bitch."

Her mind was on the party. No, her mind was on a young girl named Julie, and getting potato chips into a half dozen bowls, and trying to figure out how many hamburger patties to grill. Alex came in, bringing

November cold and the faintest sparkle of first snow in his hair. He brought with him four six-packs of additional soft drinks, a bright flash of energy and a stinging desire the instant he looked at her.

A dozen nameless resolves danced out of her head, the same ones she promised herself whenever he was out of sight. She couldn't handle this affair much longer. If he didn't love her, she had to find the pride to kick him out of her life. Only whenever he was close, she knew she'd do anything to keep him in her life again on any terms.

He shrugged out of his old leather coat. His look whipped first to the closed door of the kitchen and then back to her, assessing her toe to crown as if he could strip silk and crêpe and...control...with a look. How fast can I get you into bed? said his eyes.

"Surviving so far?" he asked brusquely.

No, she thought fleetingly. I can't continue to survive this way: not wanting you this much, and still terrified you don't love me.

Eight

I'm surviving reasonably well," Stephanie said lightly, "considering the kids have been here only twenty minutes and have already devoured about thirty pounds of potato chips. Considering there is no possible way to buy enough soda for twenty-four teenagers. Considering that I've been instructed to come in here and make buttermilk dip because Julie likes it—"

"Julie. Who's Julie?" Alex asked.

"Believe me, you'll see."

Alex bent down and peered under the table. "I see the dog has more sense than I ever gave him credit for. Think you can seriously nap through all that noise,

Walter?'' His eyes jumped back up to hers. ''I like the blouse.''

''Thank you.''

''I'd like you even better without it. What time do we get to send them all home?''

''Alex!''

He chuckled. ''All right. I'll go out there and grill hamburgers and play chaperon—''

''Not yet, you don't.'' Stephanie dropped the spoon on the counter and went over to stand in front of him. She found a fleck of lint on his red crew-neck sweater. His checked shirt had to be straightened at the collar. She pushed a flop of hair back from his forehead, even though it flopped right back down again. ''You have a lot of instructions before you go near the kids. No standing and watching the dancing. No hovering. If you see twenty-four kids completely destroying the house, try to look benign. And what car did you drive?''

''The MG.''

Her heart skipped a beat. ''You're obligated to show it to the boys. Act cool, and so forth.''

''Ah. Does my appearance pass?'' he asked wryly.

''Hmm?''

''Is there a dress code for this no one told me about?''

''Hmm?''

''Boston, if you don't keep your hands to yourself, there isn't a prayer I can be seen in public for the next half hour.''

"Don't blame me because your jeans are too tight," she said severely.

She would have dropped her hands except that he caught them and swung them around his neck. The view of the kitchen promptly dropped into the lower hemisphere. Alex's grin hovered just over her mouth, his eyes promising immediate retribution for her play. She really wasn't so wanton. It was Alex. He made her so. When she was around him, she wanted to tease. She wanted to be bold and wanton and alluring. She wanted him to laugh with her, wanted those quiet intimate smiles and the right to straighten his cowlick.

She loved him, and would have been happy to stand on her head for just one word from him that he felt the same.

He seemed more interested in watching her cheeks burn. His hands slid down her back, splayed on her hips and pulled her high and hard against him. When she didn't make the first move to stop him, he murmured, "The lady's becoming more and more bold these last few weeks, have you noticed? In fact, a man might almost be inclined to believe the lady's asking to be made love to on top of the kitchen table."

"Don't assume," she murmured back, "that the lady would say no."

Over the weeks, she'd seen his expression change just like that before. The faintest look of strain, a smile that suddenly wasn't a smile, pain hidden deep in the luminous darkness of his eyes. His lips still hovered so close that she could taste anticipation, but an instinct told her that kisses were no longer on his mind. "I need more than that, little one." His voice was little more than a husky whisper. "I need you to tell me yes. I need you to tell me exactly what you want. I need you to take that risk and trust me. Do it, Boston. Do it."

Her lips parted, yet abruptly she heard a hand jam boisterously against the swinging door. Faster than Jeff could barge in, Alex had separated from her, his hands at his sides.

"Dad! When'd you get here?"

"A minute ago, sport. How's the party?"

"Fine. Terrific. Come on in and meet Julie and the others."

Alex trailed after his son, but paused only seconds in the doorway to look back at Stephanie. The flush on her cheeks looked like a windburn. Her eyes were wild and soft. He read love in her eyes. He read yearning. Or were those just things he wanted to see? She hesitated, and then abruptly turned around, grabbing a spoon and bowl. As fast as lightning she was suddenly whipping ingredients together.

He felt despair. She saw him as an adulterer, he knew that, and that he had no defense that would pass a judge and jury. To win her, she had to know the man he was. For weeks, he'd shown her that man. For weeks, he'd played no games, applied no pressure. For weeks, he'd launched an assault simply on feelings— hers and his. And for weeks, he'd waited for the

smallest sign that she trusted him on another level, a
deeper level.

There was no sign.

At eleven-ten, a harassed Alex wandered through
the littered debris of the living room until he reached
Stephanie's side. "I thought you said they were going
home at eleven," he hissed at her ear.

"They are, they are," she murmured back, and
handed him a trayful of squashed napkins and paper
plates. "Parents are supposed to pick them up very
shortly—"

"It's all a hoax. There isn't a parent within a
hundred-mile radius of here." He raised his head to
smile calmly at a passing teenager, then whispered
mournfuly, "I'm telling you, they've all left town.
They're going to leave their kids here forever."

Stephanie chuckled. "Stop panicking and go find
Jeff. I've lost track of him, and he should be here to
say goodbye to his guests when the parents start arriving."

Her eyes wandered lovingly after him as he left her.
His humor had kept her going through a long evening, and she knew darn well he didn't mean an ounce
of his complaining. He loved the kids. His cheeks were
ruddy with cold from standing outside, patiently
showing boy after boy the engine of a '53 MG, Mark
IV TD. He'd made a rapid run to the store—how
could only twenty-four teenagers go through eighty
cans of soda in less than four hours? He'd cleaned up

spills and poured potato chips into bowls and unobtrusively plucked wallflowers off the walls, herding the
shyest teenagers back into the fold without intruding.

A half dozen times she'd wanted to go to him and
tell him simply that she loved him. He'd sparked
something during their kiss in the kitchen, an odd
uneasiness that had shimmered beneath her consciousness all evening, but there'd hardly been a second to deal with it. She surveyed her living room now
with a mixture of amusement and horror.

Arms and legs were strewn from windows to rug—
teenagers *were* all limbs at this stage. The music was
still blaring, and the noise level showed no signs of
abating. Chip bowls were empty. What hadn't been
eaten had been crunched into the carpet. Several
lampshades were askew. Truthfully, the kids had been
angels. No one had seriously abused the privilege of
the party. Naturally her living room—and dining
room, den, bathrooms and kitchen—looked as if they
qualified for federal disaster funding, but she'd
expected that.

Alex had been sidetracked in his search for his son
by a pair of freckle-faced boys. Stephanie straightened up, her eyes again scanning the room for signs of
Jeff. Actually, several of the teenagers were missing.

Two girls wandered giggling from the kitchen.
Stephanie searched the house and found one in the
extra bathroom downstairs, and in the den, she found
a couple sprawled over a chess board. Still, no Jeff. A
faint frown pleating her forehead, she checked the

basement, and then climbed the stairs. The door was open to the bathroom. No one was inside.

She ducked her head into Jeff's bedroom...and froze. Jeff and Julie were standing by his window. Both pairs of eyes were closed in a kiss. Jeff's hand was lifted to cover the girl's breast, and neither, clearly, would have heard a bomb drop, much less sensed her presence.

She turned rapidly away, so rapidly it was perhaps an excuse for the peculiar sensation of dizziness, disorientation, she felt. But it kept on. The bewildering assault of emotions had nothing to do with her son...and everything to do with him. The hallway was a blur. The next thing she remembered was Alex, standing at the base of the stairs, his hand on the banister. "Did you find him? I looked—"

"Alex, go upstairs, would you?" she said tightly. "Now."

Stephanie started collecting paper plates. Parents came and went. Jeff and Julie clambered down the stairs together. Julie's parents were suddenly there; then the girl was gone. In fact, everyone left within minutes of each other, and the stereo was finally still. Alex had joined her in the kitchen and was looking at her in a strange way when Jeff came in yawning, his grin as huge and sleepy as a bear's.

"Don't worry about all this, Mom. I'll clean up everything," he said expansively. "Actually, I'll probably do anything you want for the rest of my life.

That was the most super party I could have asked for in a million years."

"Good," Stephanie said shortly, and felt Alex's eyes on her again. She softened the curtness in her tone. "Don't worry about the cleanup, Jeff; I know you're tired. Go up to bed, your father and I—"

"I think he can help clean up," Alex interjected firmly.

They left her. She heard the roar of the vacuum cleaner from the other room, mixed with laughter between the two. A half hour later, Jeff came in to volunteer a good-night kiss. He went to bed, leaving Stephanie washing dishes and Alex standing with a towel next to her.

He said nothing for a time, but when she bent to clean the sink, which could easily have waited until morning, he abruptly stole the dishrag from her hand and tossed it onto the counter. "Spill it, Boston," he said quietly.

Her chin jerked up. "You saw where his hands were."

"On top of her sweater."

"They were still *there*."

"Honey, she was as flat as a board," Alex said dryly, trying to coax a smile.

"I don't care if she was built like a brick. They're only fourteen."

"Can't you remember puppy love?"

She turned away from grabbing the dishrag again. "Puppy love can be dangerous."

"You're taking it too seriously," he charged softly, his tenor soothing...maybe too soothing.

She whirled on him. "Alex, a girl can get pregnant if she doesn't take it just a little seriously. Don't try to give me a lecture on how 'natural' it is. I know all about exploring those natural urges. That's what we did. That's what you did."

Silence fell like deadweight. No one moved for a minute, then Alex reached over, grabbed the dishrag from her hand and threw it. It bounced off the side of the refrigerator and flipped back on the counter. She suddenly couldn't look at him. She could feel his eyes boring into hers and she could feel his anger. "You're afraid Jeff will make the same mistake we did."

"Yes!"

She made a move to go past him, but taut hands snatched her shoulders, pinned her inches from his body. Like a shimmer of heat, a warning tension radiated from him. She stared at his throat, where his Adam's apple was pulsing. "Why do I have the impression that Jeff is the last thing on your mind?" he asked sharply. "It's us, isn't it, Boston?"

"Alex..." She licked suddenly dry lips. Sadness welled in her eyes, or despair. "You didn't love me then. Not really. I always knew it. We were both kids with a pair of galloping hormones, but wanting isn't love." The swell of sadness turned into stinging tears. "It still isn't. It took me years to recover from an hour on the front seat of your MG. I can't do it again. I took one look at our son and that innocent-looking

child, and I knew I couldn't do it again. I accept..."
She took a ragged breath. "I accept that you don't
really love me, but I can't live with another relationship just based on hormones—"

His hands abruptly dropped from her shoulders.
She hurriedly brushed the tears from her cheeks,
fighting for emotional control. When her eyes blinked
clear, she could see the color had drained from Alex's
face. His jaw was granite, his eyes chips of black ice.
"You really believe that's all I feel for you? All I ever
felt for you?" he asked harshly.

Lie to him, her heart whispered. But she couldn't.
"How often have you accused me of a lack of honesty, Alex? Well, I'm being honest. If you'd felt anything else, you would have said something. You
haven't hinted at a future, at wanting..."

"A lifetime?" Alex turned, and for a moment was
motionless. Then, in a quick, impatient movement he
grabbed his leather jacket from the back of the kitchen
chair. He hesitated yet again before jamming his arms
in the sleeves, then turned back to her.

"If I never said aloud that I loved you, maybe it's
because I was afraid you wouldn't believe it. And you
wouldn't if I said it now, would you? In fact, I don't
think there's anything in hell I could ever do or say to
make you believe..." His tone changed, turning dangerously soft. "I'll return your honesty, little one.
You're right, there's no love between us. Your con-
cept of love always did seem to be very different from
mine. Does that make it easier this time? You're free

again. Believe me, I don't want your love—not as you
understand the word.''

"Alex—'' He was out the door before she could
stop him. The sound of the latch clicking shut made
her freeze. Hurt wrapped around her like a fog. In her
head echoed his words: *there's no love between us, I
don't want your love.* Her heart heard *I don't love
you,* what she'd been expecting to hear all along. What
she'd always known.

Everything suddenly hurt: her eyes, her throat, her
hands, her heart. She heard the rev of the MG's engine, then abruptly nothing. No sound dented the still,
cold night except just the tick of the clock and the
hollow beat of her heart. She'd lost him.

Snow fell, melted and fell again.

George got her through the weeks before Thanksgiving by setting her up with an auction around Rut-
land, and then another near Bretton Woods in the
White Mountain Range. Normally spring and summer were the best times to move an estate, but Stephanie was especially gifted now. She was in a mood to
sell anything to anyone. She was captured by the allure of the forbidden, of wanting things one mustn't
want, of craving to possess what one shouldn't want
to possess at all. So unconsciously she tempted their
customers and clients. She was wildly successful. Then
George took one look at her face a few days before
Thanksgiving and demanded she take a week off.

That was all right. The attic needed cleaning. And her cleaning lady did surface work, but all the cupboards needed a good scrub. The dog always needed walking. She took lots of walks. Jeff kept her busy. And the holidays were coming up; on alternate years she cooked at her father's house, so there was shopping to do.

She was very, very busy. Memories surfaced, of Alex throwing her in the leaves, making love in the basement; of his standing over her when she was sick in the hospital, waiting for Jeff; of their sudden shared laughter in the middle of the symphony. She buried the memories as fast as they happened.

Pride scabbed over the first layer of hurt. Anger worked, sometimes. The bastard. All that confusion about not believing in him . . . She did believe in him. She was the one who had risked everything. She was the one who'd laid her heart on the line, absolved him of all blame for everything in the past. She was the one who had said she loved him, and her love was evidently something he very easily tossed aside as not worth much.

She was fine when she could dredge up anger or pride. Only both were hollow emotions next to what she was missing in her life. He really wasn't coming back this time. She shouldn't want him to. It should be a very simple matter of convincing herself she didn't want him to.

The mahogany table was loaded with food—duckling, browned golden in orange sauce; cranberries; mashed potatoes and yams in honey; rolls, butter-browned and dripping; a choice of crisp salads; and glazed carrots. Sterling gleamed; Irish linen was starched and spotless; candles flickered on her father's table.

"You've outdone yourself, sweetheart," Will Randolph said warmly.

Stephanie smiled her thanks.

"Know what Dad's doing today?" Jeff heaped his plate as if he'd never seen food before.

"Eating turkey," Will suggested dryly.

"Well, yeah. But not till about six. He got tickets for the football game. And Mom?"

"Yes?"

"They're kind of combining Thanksgiving with a family celebration. Laurie's getting married."

"Laurie..."

"You know Laurie. Dad's cousin. The one with the funny-looking hair."

Stephanie didn't think she knew Laurie although actually, she might have. The Carson family tree had a dozen branches. She'd met them en masse after the wedding, and another time at Christmas, but names blurred when you were introduced to seventy-five people at once, and that was a long time ago.

Thinking about anyone with the last name of Carson at the moment wasn't the best of ideas. Out of the corner of her eye, she watched Jeff devour his dinner, politely set down his silverware and wait. His eyes pinned on hers with the hopeful expression of a child expecting the tooth fairy. His hunched shoulders were reminiscent of a racehorse at the starting gate. She sighed. "Yes."

"You mean it? Gosh, Mom..." The racehorse took its first step, then paused with a guilty look. "I should probably wait until you and Gramps finish dinner—"

Will intervened with a chuckle. "Your mother and I are nearly done, and we'll be taking a walk after dinner. Go ahead, find out what the score is. I doubt you've missed anything more than halftime."

"Well, okay, if you guys don't mind." He backed out one more cautious step, and then flew back to the living room and his football game.

Will chuckled again, shaking his head, but when he turned back to study his daughter, that smile faded. "You're not exactly in a holiday mood, sweetheart."

"Of course I am." She popped an immediate smile on, straightened her shoulders and stood up. "Pecan pie, coming up."

"Leave it for now. Unlike you, I've just had a massive dinner that needs a little walking off. Dessert can wait until we get back home."

"It's snowing, Dad...."

"Yes, I know. Get your coat."

Minutes later they were both outside. An inch of fresh snow covered the lawns and roads; the sky was a sullen gray, forecasting more. For years she and her dad had shared a walk after Thanksgiving dinner.

They always took the same route, down Park to the woods around Dartmouth's tower, then down the campus's tree-lined streets.

Bells chimed—it was four o'clock in the afternoon. The college was all but deserted for the holiday, Stephanie noted, but unfortunately there were always couples. Probably, anywhere on earth there were always couples, walking, seeking fresh air and the privacy of each other, using the cold as an excuse to keep their arms around each other, using anything as an excuse to suddenly look up and share a kiss.

"So..." her father said after he'd kept up with his daughter's killing pace for a half mile. "He's stopped coming around?"

"Alex?"

"Alex."

"Yes." Trying to disguise her loneliness, Stephanie raised her face and pretended the cold air was refreshing. "You were right, Dad," she said lightly. "Maybe I just had to try one more time to be sure, but you were right. The man just isn't for me."

"I'm glad you realized that."

"Oh, I realized that," Stephanie said bitterly.

"For one thing, if he was the kind of man to use you once..."

She stopped dead, adjusting her scarf with a violent flick over her shoulder. "Dad, he didn't use me the first time. Or this time. Get that completely out of your head. I'll probably agree with any nasty thing you want to say about Alex, but that just isn't true!"

"Mmm." Will adjusted his own scarf, much more gently. "I never did understand much of the relationship he had with Jeff," he started disparagingly.

"And that isn't the problem with him, either. He's a terrific father to Jeff and always has been," she said fiercely. "He's got a firm hand where I'm too soft. They talk together; Alex always seems to know what Jeff's feeling before I do." Stephanie tossed her head. "Believe it or not, you two even share the same values on a certain subject."

"I certainly doubt that."

"Well, it's true. We had a furious argument one day. The idiot had this idea Jeff was going to Dartmouth no matter what our son wanted."

"He did, did he?"

"He says he wants something better for Jeff. As if he had something to be ashamed of for being a mechanic... For Lord's sake, look at him! He's made so much of his life—"

"But then, he was alway sensitive about his background," Will said smoothly.

"He hasn't any reason to be sensitive about his background. Fact is, he's an inverse snob," Stephanie said stiffly.

"Hmm. Of course, he had reason to be sensitive about it once upon a time, knowing he couldn't provide for you—"

"He could provide for four wives at the moment," Stephanie said flatly. "That was never an issue, anyway. I don't need anyone to provide for me now."

"He probably wanted you to need him, and knew you didn't. You don't need anyone, sweetheart. Believe me, I understand, because I holed up after your mother died and got along just fine," Will said gruffly.

Stephanie glanced at her father. Her oldest memories were of her father by himself, reading at night in his study, and of a terrible loneliness she'd sensed even as a child. Her father wasn't looking at her, but straight ahead at the Georgian architecture of the old Baker Memorial Building.

"We all need someone," she said quietly.

"But you don't need him," Will said encouragingly. "All he's ever done is hurt you."

"Yes." Tears pricked her eyes, damn them. "You know, I even admitted to him that I was to blame for what went wrong with us. Even for the redhead. And I was to blame, Dad. I wasn't mature enough for marriage, for a commitment of that kind." She sighed fiercely. "Well, forget it. Never again."

"Good."

"And I do mean never. He's completely out of my system."

"Good," Will echoed. "You never needed that man. For anything."

More tears pricked her eyes; she blinked hard. Her father was so right. She didn't need Alex for finances, for security. She wasn't helpless anymore, floundering with every little crisis. She didn't need any man to define her values for her, to lead her into choices. She could make her own.

Only her father was *so wrong*. She needed Alex to make her laugh. She needed him to argue with, to make her feel. She needed him to love.

Why couldn't she make herself stop thinking about him?

"And besides, the man would have been like an albatross. He needed you too much," her father mentioned absently.

"Alex?" She turned startled eyes to her father. "What are you talking about? Alex never needed me for anything. Ever."

"Didn't he?" Will fluffed off snow from his coat shoulders. "Perhaps not. Usually a man who's had a tough road alone especially needs a woman, someone he knows will be there when the chips are down. On the other hand, who cares? He'll find someone. Don't even think about it."

She thought about it—about Alex's sensitivity to his background, about his damnable pride, about the way he'd forced her to grow and express her feelings...and suddenly about how little she'd given back to him. Alex was open and blunt and strong. She never thought of him as vulnerable. How could he be vulnerable? He was successful at everything he did. He didn't need anyone to tell him that.

"He had the nerve to call me twice these past two weeks," Will Randolph said disgustedly. "I just told him to leave you alone."

"He called?"

"Certainly. I told him to leave you be. That was what you wanted, wasn't it?"

They suddenly seemed to be back at her father's place. Will reached the top step first, and paused a moment to stomp the snow from his boots. Before Stephanie could reach the door, though, he'd quietly blocked the entrance. He very badly wanted to let her in, where he knew she'd been warm and safe, where he could perhaps distract her a little longer with a glass of wine and a quiet game of chess.

Except that a father only had so many chances to take back the mistakes he'd made. "Sweetheart," he said gently, "what I would like you to do is go home, get the dog and bring him back here. And bring Jeff's things back here for an overnight as well."

"Pardon?"

"You can be in Boston by seven-thirty."

"If I were going to Boston."

"Oh, you're going to Boston," her father assured her. "The only damn thing I can't figure out is why you're still here."

Nine

The moment she got off Interstate 93, Stephanie was lost. From the years her father had been a professor at Boston U. she'd learned how easy it was to be lost in Boston, particularly near the neighborhood where Alex had grown up. It had been ages since she'd gone to the Carson home, but she discovered nothing had changed. Row after row of two-story frame houses all looked alike. They were old and of the same weathered gray and brown, and clustered on tangled streets wrapped in cold, wet fog.

She found the street but still couldn't identify the house, until she spotted Alex's red MG parked on the road, jammed in between car after car. She had to drive a block before she found a place for her own.

She parked, shoved her keys into her purse, took out lipstick and looked up. You're nuts, Stephanie informed her image in the rearview mirror. First of all, he doesn't want to see you. He all but told you he didn't love you. And second, no sane woman would voluntarily interrupt a Carson family gathering.

Yes. She applied lipstick, blush, tightened the pins holding her hair in a coil, popped an antacid mint in her mouth and stepped out of the car. Her suede boots promptly sank into slush and a bitter wind slashed open her red wool coat. By the time she walked the block to his parents' house her stomach was in knots and she was freezing. Still, when she reached their front door, her hands locked firmly at her sides because they refused to reach for the knocker.

The Carsons... She just wasn't prepared for them. Unfortunately she'd never been prepared for the Carson family. She'd grown up in a household where dinners were inevitably formal and voices were never raised. The Carsons were noisy, garrulous, overtly and effusively affectionate with each other. They argued at the top of their lungs and laughed just as boisterously.

She'd always been overwhelmed by them, and Alex's mother had taken one look and disliked her years before. "Haughty" was the word Stephanie had overheard. How that single word had hurt.

She would have loved them, if she'd known how. She loved the way they talked and teased and yelled and took loving each other for granted. As for joining in, though, she'd never known how. They were so very different.

His father worked in a factory; his mother was the only Carson of few words, but her life was spent taking care of people. A sister was a clerk in a store. A brother was a line foreman somewhere. None of the Carsons had been eaten up with ambition the way Alex was, but they were happy people. From the very first time he'd brought home his Boston Brahmin, she could sense their judgment of her. She was responsible for Alex's being unhappy with the status quo. She was the one who'd lured him into trouble, with her champagne hair and long legs, then she was the one who had deserted him.

She couldn't possibly go in there and face them again.

And if she had the choice... But on the long drive here, she'd discovered she had no choices. His family were part of Alex. Alex was hopelessly part of her. She had to put herself in a frame of mind to move mountains.

She lifted her chin and rapped on the door. There was no answer, but then the incredibly high noise level inside was seeping through the closed door. Undoubtedly no one had heard her. She turned the knob and pushed, then waited for the steel wool to climb off the walls of her stomach. She was here to move mountains, and it wouldn't do to be sick on Mrs. Carson's front porch.

She arranged a smile on her face and poked her head in the door. The dimly lit hall led directly to the living room, where she could see part of an old wooden table covered with a white tablecloth. The women were whisking to and fro, gabbing a mile a minute as they carted leftovers and dishes to the kitchen. Children were chortling as they raced up and down the stairs. Men's husky voices echoed from a far room. It sounded as if there were a hundred of them.

Her palms went damp with helpless nerves. Everyone she saw had the Carson dark eyes and clear skin and the same thick, healthy hair, but beyond that, names eluded her. There was a Peg, a Martha, a Jimmy. Bette, Phil, an uncle they called Whitt, Bob and Robbie...but except for Alex's parents she couldn't conceivably connect a name to a face.

And then she saw his mother, alone for only an instant in the living room, bending to pick up the last of the glasses from the table. She wore an old print dress—she probably had bought it years ago. His mother looked worn, but she hadn't changed. Clothes didn't matter to her—the old values did. Her stern profile could quell the most rambunctious toddler. A quiet word from her and the Carson men jumped. Her capacity to love was infinite, but Stephanie was well aware that capacity had never been extended to her.

"Mary Agnes?" she said softly.

Alex's mother looked up, without the least sign that the presence of Stephanie startled her. Nothing ever surprised Mary Agnes, but it was strange, how in a house full of noise there was suddenly silence. Old judgments passed between them. Stephanie could read the loyalty of a mother in her eyes, the rage for anyone who would dare to hurt one of her own—twice. She met his mother's gaze, unflinching, but she could feel the older woman scan her red coat, her suede boots, her face. Mary Agnes intensely searched her face.

"I'm going to see Alex," Stephanie stated quietly.

Braced for a confrontation, she was startled when his mother only nodded, and then shook her head with a maternal cluck. "Too thin," she scolded. "Don't take care of yourself. I told you that a long time ago. And standing there with snow on your feet." She clucked again. "Get your coat off, sit down now. Don't be standing there like I'm going to eat you. You sit. I'll get Laurie to fetch Alex for you."

Hearing her name, a frizzy blonde cocked her head from the kitchen doorway, her dark eyes blinking in surprise. "Stephanie?" Her smile was open and friendly as she whirled in the room, extending her hand. "Remember me? I think the only time I actually met you was just before you and Alex eloped years ago, but I can still remember."

"No time to stand around talking. She needs something to drink," Mary Agnes told her. "She's colder than a stone."

"No," Stephanie said swiftly.

"I'll get it; I'll get it—"

"Really, I..." A rapidly poured glass of white wine was in her hand before she could stop it.

"And when she's finished that, you get Alex for her," Mary Agnes announced, and continued to the kitchen with the tray of glasses as if nothing unusual had happened. Stephanie let out an uneasy breath, bewilderingly aware that she'd been welcomed, Mary Agnes style. Adrenaline was still pumping up her veins, with no place to go. She'd expected a battle, a brusque cold shoulder at the very best.

"Stephanie?"

Still standing in her coat, she turned back to the friendly face of the frizzy blonde, and tried to concentrate on remembering her. The woman could only be a year or two younger than she was. They were about the same height, but the mop of overly curly blond hair was surely distinctive in this family. Surely she would know her if she'd met her before.

"Laurie," the other woman repeated with a little laugh. "You really don't remember me, do you? Relax, sit down a minute. You want me to take your coat?"

"No, thank you. I..." Stephanie took a breath. "I just want Alex."

"Thank God," the blonde said lightly, and perched on the worn end of a couch.

"Pardon?"

Laurie chuckled. "Someone's got to straighten him out. Heaven knows the whole family's tried these past few weeks. He's always been my favorite cousin, but

I'll tell you... Never mind that, just relax for a minute." She snapped her fingers suddenly. "I know why you don't remember me." She pointed to her head. "I wasn't blond when I first met you; does that help? When I get depressed, I change the color of my hair. Disgrace of the family, that. I've been frosted, brunette, streaked, blond... went through a long period as a redhead when I was in high school."

"Redhead," Stephanie echoed.

"*Now* you remember, don't you? I thought the whole family would kill me. I ran away to Alex. He was the only one who ever understood...but no," her eyebrows fluttered up, "you couldn't remember that. You weren't at home when I ran off to try and live with you two. Alex sent me home anyway, but I can still remember that little apartment you had, and how pretty you had made everything."

The blonde cocked her head, eyes radiating compassion. "You've turned white as a sheet," she said gently. "Drink your wine. Don't mind me for talking so much; it's one of the worst of family traits, as you probably already know. Except for Aunt Mary, of course."

"Yes." Stop talking just for a minute, Stephanie wanted to say. Please. I have to think. I very badly have to think.

The blonde paused, then smiled again. "Don't feel awkward. It couldn't have been easy for you, coming here. We all know what happened the first time, of course, but he hasn't said a word these past few

months. We guessed it was you; that wasn't hard, the
way he's looked and acted. But no one's going to say
a word against you, please believe that. In fact..." She
hesitated again, her cheeks suddenly the color of a
peach. "I do talk too much, don't I? And it must have
sounded like I was prying. Look, I'll just go get him."

"No." Stephanie set down the full glass of wine,
and for a few seconds closed her eyes. Images of redheads danced in her head. Over the years she'd imagined dozens of redheads: sultry ones with waist-length
auburn hair, freckled ones with a copper cap. She'd
imagined long red hair, short red hair, every possible
manner of redhead except one with a frizz of unmanageable curls topping a cousin's guileless bright eyes.
"No," she repeated, stronger now. "I'll find Alex."

"Are you sure?" Laurie said hesitantly.

"Believe me, very sure."

It was only a short walk down the hall to the sound
of men's voices. The back room was traditionally the
Carson men's refuge. She paused in the doorway,
vaguely aware of thick cigar smoke, the blare of a
football game, the lazy inclusion of four-letter words
in conversation that Mary Agnes would never have
allowed in other rooms in the house.

She was aware, yet she wasn't. A slow, steady fire
was licking up her veins, gaining momentum with
every second that passed. Her palms were no longer
damp. The acid in her stomach didn't dare churn.

Two pairs of eyes turned to her, then a half dozen.
Conversations filtered off gradually, before dark eyes

whipped up to hers from across the room. He was wearing dark pants, a dark red shirt. He looked like hell. Bitter lines around his mouth and eyes glowed white with exhaustion under the artificial light. No one seemed to have scolded him into a fresh shave. He was gaunt and his eyes were shadowed. Stephanie felt the flames lick higher, hotter, more intensely.

She had never understood more than at the moment how damn much Alex needed to be loved. And she had never, ever, been more furious with another human being.

He didn't move in that instant he saw her. He couldn't. He wasn't absolutely positive she was there, that he wasn't imagining the ghost of fragile perfume, the delicate female form in the doorway, the passionate blaze of blue eyes. His own private hell could have conjured up the image. His mind had thought up the image often enough in the past few weeks.

When he didn't move in that first instant, Stephanie felt the ghost of despair, a terrifying bleakness...but rage gave her courage. Before he could possibly say anything, she turned on her heel and walked out. Indifferent, would he have her believe? The hell he was. And there were ways and means to budge Alex.

She passed one bedroom, two. All coats were kept on his parents' beds during family gatherings. She had no trouble identifying his leather jacket. Riffling through the pockets, she snatched his car keys and was

winging down the hall toward the front door before a
minute could pass.

Outside, she whisked down the driveway as fast as
she could on the slushy pavement, then slid into the
black leather seat of the MG. The thing had a clutch;
she hadn't handled a stick shift in years, but it didn't
take much to turn a key and loudly rev an engine. She
jerked the thing out of the parking space, then gunned
it until she was backed up in front of the Carson
house. She revved the engine a second time. Loudly.

Not surprising her a bit, the front door slammed
open. Alex was still trying to put an arm in his jacket
sleeve.

She revved the engine a third time. Within seconds,
the passenger door was jerked open. "Boston, what
the hell are you doing?"

From looking half-dead minutes before, Alex had
suddenly come alive. His eyes were snapping and he
had run his fingers through his thick dark hair. Won-
ders, what an MG Mark IV TD could do. There were
only a hundred or so of them in the world. They were
very effective.

"It's really my car," she said evenly. "I lost my in-
nocence in this car. I made a baby in this car. It's mine,
and it's past time I claimed what's mine, and you
might as well get in, Alex. If you don't, I'm going
back in that house and tell your entire family that you
made me pregnant again."

He sucked in his breath for a second, staring at her.
She wasn't ready to face the look in his eyes yet. In-

difference, anger, irritation, rejection... She didn't want to know. For that instant, she even convinced herself she didn't care, and then he abruptly folded his muscular frame inside and closed the door. She breathed again. Those fires flamed again.

"You're not," he said flatly, but there was a rasp of a question in his voice.

"I'm not," she snapped, "but don't think I wouldn't tell every Carson third cousin from here to Poughkeepsie if you don't strap in."

"Boston. I don't know when you took up drinking—"

"I have certainly not been drinking."

"Then you've gone nuts?"

"You bet I have." Tears suddenly glistened in her eyes. Damn. She pushed the car in gear and let up on the clutch—too quickly. The car stalled. "I am furious." She turned the key again. The car stalled again. A car and then two backed up behind her.

"Boston. Don't cry."

"I am not crying. I am furious. With you."

"Let me drive—"

"I'm driving. And you're just... you're just going to sit."

He sat. He didn't say a word when she stalled at stoplights. Or when she ground gears downshifting. He didn't do a damn thing but look at her the entire drive. Twice she thought he was going to say something, but he didn't.

She wasn't at all sure how or why she ended up at
the wharf. The sea was wild, all black water and gray
foam slamming against the docks. The old buildlings
nearby were deserted for the holiday. They were
weathered and peeling, snow sticking in their cracks as
the ocean gusted in a night blend of wind and snow
and fog. The air was spiced with winter and salt wind
and fish. Boston in November never smelled any other
way. Far in the distance, the lonely neon lights of a
restaurant flashed on and off, but there was no one
around.

She turned off the engine, leaned back and stared
straight ahead. "You're going home with me," she
announced. Where was the fire when she needed it?
She meant to sound assertive and forceful and angry
and indomitable, but somehow her voice came out
trembling.

"Boston—"

"Or I'm going home with you. I don't care which.
Alex, I've had enough, and there isn't the least point
in your arguing."

He wasn't arguing, but he suddenly leaned over. It
had only taken seconds for their breath to fog up the
windows. The MG had never had a lot of spare space,
but it suddenly became a very small cocoon that iso-
lated them from the rest of the world. The cocoon was
filled only with a woman who was trying to be angry
and a man with deep, dark eyes, who was stealing the
gloves from her hands, pushing off her scarf, making
her look at him.

He wasn't angry. He wasn't rejecting her. She'd already figured that out on the drive here, but she'd never expected the vulnerable look to his mouth. Still she hadn't forgotten what agonies he'd caused her. "To hell with you, Alex. Do you hear me?"

"I hear you."

"I mean it. I've had completely enough. For one thing, you're never going to convince me you don't love me—"

"I adore you, Steph. I like you, love you, respect you, want you, need you, adore you. Boston, I'm sorry. So sorry. I was wrong—"

She heard the pain in his voice. It was a slow, aching cadence of pain, but it was her eyes that filled with tears. Soft tears came this time, just enough to make the whole world brilliant.

"That's just it, you know," she whispered hoarsely. "This whole business of being wrong. I can't seem to stop making mistakes, Alex. I wish I could promise you it would never happen again, but I know it will. You're just going to have to forgive me. You're just going to have to forget everything."

"I never blamed you," he said fiercely. "I was the one to blame for everything. Not you. I thought it was you who couldn't forget." Haunted eyes seared hers. "I couldn't make you trust me again. I had no way to build trust between us, not believing what you do." He added harshly, "And I have no proof that I never slept with that redhead."

"Don't you?" Her eyes suddenly blazed aquamarine. His cousin's face swept into her mind. Proof wasn't there, only guesses. And that kind of proof suddenly didn't matter. She suddenly understood how little it had ever mattered. "You're the only man I ever met who could use a daily shaking, Alex. You and your damned pride. All this time, and you could simply have told me—"

"If you would have believed me. I didn't have a reason in hell to think you'd trust anything I'd say."

"Your proof was your word," she said furiously. "How dare you think I never valued it!"

"Steph—"

"No. You listen to me." She gestured helplessly with her hands. "At the time, I was seventeen and ugly-pregnant and horribly aware I was failing you as a mate, a woman, a wife. Hush!" she said fiercely when he opened his mouth. "I know what I felt then. I left you because I had to. It had nothing to do with another woman. It had to do with you and me. Believe that."

"I . . ."

"Will you hush?"

He hushed.

The haunted look was easing from his eyes, yet suddenly she couldn't stop trembling. "Alex, yes, I hurt like hell at the thought you'd been unfaithful. But not like you're thinking. I wasn't judging you for turning to someone else, not after everything I'd put you through. I was trying to tell you that I know you're human, no more and no less human than I am. We're both fallible. I was trying to give you a gift, not a judgment. And I very badly need that gift back from you, because we've nowhere to go at all if you can't forgive my being so terribly wrong—"

"Don't be foolish. I love you," he said suddenly. "I love you, Boston. There's nothing you could ever do that I wouldn't forgive you for."

He fell silent, his eyes searching hers. There was a last trace of rigid tension in his muscles that suddenly eased. His mouth softened, but there was no smile, just an intense vibration between them, a hum of love no one else could hear, silent promises no one else could possibly understand. His grave eyes flickered away from her then, first to her mouth, then to her hair. He reached up and started slipping out the pins one by one.

"Alex—" she warned.

"You're not through talking?"

"I'm not through talking."

"Then talk," he encouraged her.

"We're going to have no more problems like that," she informed him. "One of us in this car clearly needs to learn how to express his feelings more openly. I'm not saying that's an easy thing to do, but it can be learned with the right kind of teacher. A man one trusts and believes in from the heart makes a very good kind of teacher."

A slow, lazy smile suddenly spread over his face. "Yes, you've learned, haven't you?" he murmured.

When the last pin was gone, he turned the crank on the window an inch and tossed them outside in the snow.

"And another thing, you're going to buy me more hairpins."

"Yes." He frowned before reaching for her. Between them was a gearshift. Affecting their closeness were bucket seats. He combed his fingers through her hair while he considered the problem.

"And another thing. This business about Jeff and being a mechanic, which never had anything to do with Jeff being a mechanic. It was about you. Being proud of what you've done with your life..."

"Yes." He swung her legs over the gearshift, then lifted her to his lap. Amazing, how two grown people could have so many bulky limbs. Stephanie, of course, had always been agile. Logistics had never been so perfect to wrap his arms around her and seal promises with kisses. His lips started with the thoughtful frown between her eyes, moved down to the tip of her nose, then claimed her mouth.

Claim was the feeling. Possession. He claimed her softness, her sweetness, her understanding. He could compete in any man's world and did. It had never meant much without her to come home to. His pride was linked to Stephanie. He needed her.

Her mouth was sweet and giving, and her lips turned warm under his insistent, tender assault. He wooed with the kiss as he'd always wanted to woo her, promising he would protect her, shield her, coax her to grow and feel and love. The boy had been powerless to do any of those things. The man felt all power as he took in the nectar of her response. She was made of so much love.

She broke free only when she was breathless, and then only moved inches away. "Alex. You mustn't get ideas. You know it's nearly impossible."

"Yes. Shift your leg this way, honey."

She shifted her leg. "We're not done talking. We have to talk about parents, your parents and my father. And Jeff—"

"Yes."

"You're not listening."

"Yes." He punched the lock button on both doors, then reached for her.

Jeff tried unobtrusively to scratch his neck, where the starched collar was chafing. The chapel was stifling, which didn't help. Outside, a winter wind was whipping up a pure white Christmas. He took another look at his mother and father, but they weren't even listening to the preacher. They were looking only at each other. He leaned toward his grandfather. "They wouldn't be together right now if it weren't for me, you know."

"You think so?" Will Randolph gave his grandson a wry look. He'd just been giving himself credit for the two standing at the altar. His eyes narrowed while studying his son-in-law. Nothing wrong with the man in a tux; he had the shoulders and the posture to pull one off, but nothing ever seemed to make the man's hair look tame.

His eyes wandered across the aisle to the Carsons. The father was the spitting image of Alex, give or take the silver hair. But the mother—Mary Agnes—was dressed in blue crêpe, and had on a dour expression. The woman irritated Will. He couldn't read her, and he was damned if anyone or anything was going to mar his daughter's day.

Stephanie floated down the aisle moments later. Will's eyes misted and averted from the two newlyweds when they shared their own version of a wedding kiss just outside the door. He stepped out into the aisle and abruptly encountered Mary Agnes Carson.

The two sized each other up in the space of a second. Both stiffened their shoulders, brought up their chins. They didn't see each other again until they both had a glass of champagne in their hands, and again they both bristled ... until Mary Agnes bent forward and motioned at him toward Alex and Stephanie— neither of whom seemed the least aware that anyone else was in the room with them.

"You give them eight months or nine?" Mary Agnes demanded of Will Randolph.

Will's eyes chilled. "If you think my daughter..."

"Oh, I think your daughter. And I know my son as well. And I don't much care as long as I get another grandchild and soon."

"A girl this time," Will said swiftly.

"Another boy," Mary Agnes contradicted.

Will found a folded dollar in his pocket. The bet was sealed.

In time, they both won.

Silhouette Desire
COMING NEXT MONTH

TREASURE HUNT—Maura Seger
When Lucas and Emily dove for sunken diamonds, the modern-day pirates after them weren't the only danger. They recovered the treasure, but they lost their hearts—to each other.

THE MYTH AND THE MAGIC—Christine Flynn
Combining Stephanie's impulsiveness and Adam's scientific logic meant nothing but trouble. Mythical beast or archaeological abnormality—could the fossil they found lead to the magic of love?

LOVE UNDERCOVER—Sandra Kleinschmit
After reporter Brittany Daniels and detective Gabe Spencer got used to the idea that they needed one another to crack a case, they soon discovered that work and play needn't be mutually exclusive.

DESTINY'S DAUGHTER—Elaine Camp
Years before, Banner's mother had deserted her family for the love of another man. Yuri was that man's son. Could they let the past they couldn't control destroy their chance for a future?

MOMENT OF TRUTH—Suzanne Simms
Michael just couldn't get Alexa out of his mind. Her flamboyance wreaked havoc with his stuffy pin-striped orthodoxy, but when they kissed they had to face the facts: this was love.

SERENDIPITY SAMANTHA—Jo Ann Algermissen
She was an inventor, and nothing could distract her from her work until she met Jack Martin, and a flash of genius became a flash of desire.

AVAILABLE NOW:

LOVEPLAY
Diana Palmer

FIRESTORM
Doreen Owens Malek

JULIET
Ashley Summers

SECRET LOVE
Nancy John

FOOLISH PLEASURE
Jennifer Greene

TEXAS GOLD
Joan Hohl